HORRID HENRY'S WICKED WAYS

FRANCESCA SIMON

HORRID HENRY'S WICKED WAYS

Illustrated by
Tony Ross

Orion
Children's Books

First published in Great Britain in 2005
by Orion Children's Books
Paperback edition first published in 2006
by Orion Children's Books
a division of the Orion Publishing Group Ltd
Orion House
5 Upper St Martin's Lane
London WC2H 9EA

3 5 7 9 10 8 6 4 2

A catalogue record for this book
is available from the British Library.

Printed in Italy

ISBN-10 1 84255 524 3
ISBN-13 978 1 84255 524 8

www.orionbooks.co.uk

CONTENTS

Grandma   Dad   Mum

Fluffy

Henry   Peter   Steve

HORRID HENRY'S FAMILY

Great-Aunt Greta

Aunt Ruby

Fang

Vera

Paul

Polly

Henry

HORRID HENRY
AND THE
COMFY BLACK CHAIR

Ah, Saturday! Best day of the week, thought Horrid Henry, flinging off the covers and leaping out of bed. No school! No homework! A day of TV heaven! Mum and Dad liked sleeping in on a Saturday. So long as Henry and Peter were quiet they could watch TV until Mum and Dad woke up.

Horrid Henry could picture it now. He would stretch out in the comfy black chair, grab the remote control, and switch on the TV. All his favourite shows were on today: *Rapper Zapper, Mutant Max*, and *Gross-Out*. If he hurried he would be just in time for *Rapper Zapper.*

He thudded down the stairs and flung open the sitting room door. A horrible sight met his eyes.

There, stretched out on the comfy black chair and clutching the remote control, was his younger brother, Perfect Peter.

Henry gasped. How could this be? Henry always got downstairs first. The TV was already on. But it was not switched to *Rapper Zapper*. A terrible tinkly tune trickled out of the TV. Oh no! It was the world's most boring show, *Daffy and her Dancing Daisies*.

'Switch the channel!' ordered Henry. '*Rapper Zapper*'s on.'

'That's a horrid, nasty programme,' said Perfect Peter, shuddering. He held tight to the remote.

'I said switch the channel!' hissed Henry.

'I won't!' said Peter. 'You know the rules. The first one downstairs gets to sit in the comfy black chair and decides what to watch. And I want to watch *Daffy*.'

Henry could hardly believe his ears. Perfect Peter was . . . refusing to obey an order?

'NO!' screamed Henry. 'I hate that show. I want to watch *Rapper Zapper*!'

'Well, I want to watch *Daffy*,' said Perfect Peter.

'But that's a baby show,' said Henry.

'Dance, my daisies, dance!' squealed the revolting Daffy.

'La, la la la la!' trilled the daisies.

'La, la la la la!' sang Peter.

'Baby, baby!' taunted Henry. If only he could get Peter to run upstairs crying then *he* could get the chair.

'Peter is a baby, Peter is a baby!' jeered Henry.

Peter kept his eyes glued to the screen.

Horrid Henry could stand it no longer. He pounced on Peter, snatched the remote, and pushed Peter onto the floor. He was Rapper Zapper liquidizing a pesky android.

'AAAAAH!' screamed Perfect Peter. 'MUUUMMM!'

Horrid Henry leaped into the comfy black chair and switched channels.

'Grrrrrr!' growled Rapper Zapper, blasting a baddie.

'DON'T BE HORRID, HENRY!' shouted Mum, storming through the door. 'GO TO YOUR ROOM!'

'NOOOO!' wailed Henry. 'Peter started it!'

'NOW!' screamed Mum.

'La, la la la la!' trilled the daisies.

BUZZZZZZZZZ.

Horrid Henry switched off the alarm. It was six a.m. the following Saturday. Henry was taking no chances. Even if he had to grit his teeth and watch *Rise and Shine* before *Gross-Out* started it was worth it. And he'd seen the coming attractions for today's *Gross-Out*: who could eat the most cherry pie in five minutes while blasting the other contestants with a goo-shooter. Henry couldn't wait.

There was no sound from Peter's room. Ha, ha, thought Henry. He'll have to sit on the lumpy sofa and watch what *I* want to watch.

Horrid Henry skipped into the sitting room. And stopped.

'Remember, children, always eat with a knife and fork!' beamed a cheerful presenter. It was *Manners with Maggie*. There was Perfect Peter in his slippers and dressing gown, stretched out on the comfy black chair. Horrid Henry felt sick. Another Saturday ruined! He had to watch *Gross-Out*! He just had to.

13

Horrid Henry was just about to push Peter off the chair when he stopped. Suddenly he had a brilliant idea.

'Peter! Mum and Dad want to see you. They said it's urgent!'

Perfect Peter leaped off the comfy black chair and dashed upstairs.

Tee hee, thought Horrid Henry.

ZAP!

'Welcome to *GROSS-OUT*!' shrieked the presenter, Marvin the Maniac. 'Boy, will you all be feeling sick today! It's GROSS! GROSS! GROSS!'

'Yeah!' said Horrid Henry. This was great!

Perfect Peter reappeared.

'They didn't want me,' said Peter. 'And they're cross because I woke them up.'

'They told me they did,' said Henry, eyes glued to the screen.

Peter stood still.

'Please give me the chair back, Henry.'

Henry didn't answer.

'I had it first,' said Peter.

'Shut up, I'm trying to watch,' said Henry.

'Ewwwwww, gross!' screamed the TV audience.

'I was watching *Manners with Maggie*,' said Peter. 'She's showing how to eat soup without slurping.'

'Tough,' said Henry. 'Oh, gross!' he chortled, pointing at the screen.

Peter hid his eyes.

'Muuuuummmmmmmm!' shouted Peter. 'Henry's being mean to me!'

Mum appeared in the doorway.

She looked furious.

'Henry, go to your room!' shouted Mum. 'We were trying to sleep. Is it too much to ask to be left in peace one morning a week?'

'But Peter —'

Mum pointed to the door.

'Out!' said Mum.

'It's not fair!' howled Henry, stomping off.

ZAP!

'And now Kate, our guest manners expert, will demonstrate the proper way to butter toast.'

Henry slammed the door behind him as hard as he could. Peter had got the comfy black chair for the very last time.

BUZZZZZZZ.

Horrid Henry switched off the alarm. It was two a.m. the *following* Saturday. The *Gross-Out* Championships were on in the morning. He grabbed his pillow and duvet and sneaked out of the room. He was taking no chances. Tonight he would *sleep* in the comfy black chair. After all, Mum and Dad had never said how *early* he could get up.

Henry tiptoed out of his room into the hall.

All quiet in Peter's room.

All quiet in Mum and Dad's.

Henry crept down the stairs and carefully opened the sitting room door. The room was pitch black. Better not turn on the light, thought Henry. He felt his way along the wall until his fingers touched the back of the comfy black chair. He felt around the top. Ah, there was the remote. He'd sleep with that under his pillow, just to be safe.

Henry flung himself onto the chair and landed on something lumpy.

'AHHHHHHHHH!' screamed Henry.

'AHHHHHHHHH!' screamed the Lump.

'HELP!' screamed Henry and the Lump.

Feet pounded down the stairs.

'What's going on down there?' shouted Dad, switching on the light.

Henry blinked.

'Henry jumped on my head!' snivelled a familiar voice beneath him.

'Henry, what are you doing?' said Dad. 'It's two o'clock in the morning!'

Henry's brain whirled. 'I thought I heard a burglar so I crept down to keep watch.'

'Henry's lying!' said Peter, sitting up. 'He came down because he wanted the comfy black chair.'

'Liar!' said Henry. 'And what were *you* doing down here?'

'I couldn't sleep and I didn't want to wake you, Dad,' said Peter. 'So I came down as quietly as I could to get a drink of water. Then I felt sleepy and lay down for a moment. I'm very sorry, Dad, it will never happen again.'

'All right,' said Dad, stifling a yawn. 'From now on, you are not to come down here before seven a.m. or there will be no TV for a week! Is that clear?'

'Yes, Dad,' said Peter.

'Yeah,' muttered Henry.

He glared at Perfect Peter.

Perfect Peter glared at Horrid Henry. Then they both went upstairs to their bedrooms and closed the doors.

'Goodnight!' called Henry cheerfully. 'My, I'm sleepy.'

But Henry did not go to bed. He needed to think.

He *could* wait until everyone was asleep and sneak back down. But what if he got caught? No TV for a week would be unbearable.

But what if he missed the *Gross-Out* Championships? And never found out if Tank Thomas or Tapioca Tina won the day? Henry shuddered. There had to be a better way.

Ahh! He had it! He would set his clock ahead and make sure he was first down. Brilliant! *Gross-Out* here I come, he thought.

But wait. What if Peter had the *same* brilliant idea? That would spoil everything. Henry had to double-check.

Henry opened his bedroom door. The coast was clear. He tiptoed out and sneaked into Peter's room.

There was Peter, sound asleep. And there was his clock. Peter hadn't changed the time. Phew.

And then Henry had a truly wicked idea. It was so evil, and so horrid, that for a moment even he hesitated. But hadn't Peter been horrible and selfish, stopping Henry watching his favourite shows? He certainly had. And wouldn't it be great if Peter got into trouble, just for once?

Perfect Peter rolled over. 'La, la la la la,' he warbled in his sleep.

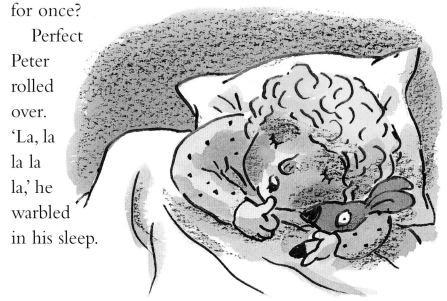

That did it. Horrid Henry moved Peter's clock an hour ahead. Then Henry sneaked downstairs and turned up the TV's volume as loud as it would go.

Finally, he opened Mum and Dad's door, and crept back to bed.

'IT'S GROW AND SHOW! THE VEGETABLE SHOW FOR TINIES! JUST LOOK AT ALL THESE LOVELY VEGETABLES!'

The terrible noise boomed through the house, blasting Henry out of bed.

'HENRY!' bellowed Dad. 'Come here this instant!'

Henry sauntered into his parents' bedroom.

21

'What is it?' he asked, yawning loudly.

Mum and Dad looked confused.

'Wasn't that you watching TV downstairs?'

'No,' said Henry, stretching. 'I was asleep.'

Mum looked at Dad.

Dad looked at Mum.

'You mean *Peter* is downstairs watching TV at six a.m.?'

Henry shrugged.

'Send Peter up here this minute!' said Dad.

For once Henry did not need to be asked twice. He ran downstairs and burst into the sitting room.

'I grew carrots!'

'I grew string beans!'

'Peter! Mum and Dad want to see you right away!' said Henry.

Peter didn't look away from *Grow and Show.*

'PETER! Dad asked me to send you up!'

'You're just trying to trick me,' said Peter.

'You'd better go or you'll be in big trouble,' said Henry.

'Fool me once, shame on you. Fool me twice, shame on me,' said Peter. 'I'm not moving.'

'Now, just look at all these beautiful tomatoes Timmy's grown,' squealed the TV.

'Wow,' said Peter.

'Don't say I didn't warn you,' said Henry.

'PETER!' bellowed Dad. 'NO TV FOR A
MONTH! COME HERE THIS MINUTE!'

Perfect Peter burst into tears. He jumped from the
chair and crept out of the room.

Horrid Henry sauntered over to the comfy black chair and stretched out. He picked up the remote and switched channels.

ZAP!

Rapper Zapper stormed into the spaceship and pulverized some alien slime.

'Way to go, Rapper Zapper!' shrieked Horrid Henry. Soon *Gross-Out* would be on. Wasn't life sweet?

dear Mum and Dad

I want more pockit money and I want it now. **Or else.**

Henry

Henry
what have you done to <u>deserve</u> more pocket money?
Mum.

I didn't kick Peter today and I only called him Pongy-Pants and Mega-Stink twice. So I think I deserve a medal **AND** loads of loot
Henry

HORRID HENRY'S
HOUSE

Stop calling me a worm.
And your room is smelly.

Not as smelly as you.

Meanie

Poo-breath

HORRID HENRY
AND THE
FANGMANGLER

orrid Henry snatched his skeleton bank and tried to twist open the trap door. Mum was taking him to Toy Heaven tomorrow. At last Henry would be able to buy the toy of his dreams: a Dungeon Drink kit. Ha ha ha – the tricks he'd play on his family, substituting their drinks for Dungeon stinkers.

Best of all, Moody Margaret would be green with envy. She wanted a Dungeon Drink kit too, but she didn't have any money. He'd have one first, and no way was Margaret ever going to play with it. Except for buying the occasional sweet and a few comics, Henry had been saving his money for weeks.

Perfect Peter peeked round the door.

'I've saved £7.53,' said Peter proudly, jingling his piggy bank.

'More than enough to buy my nature kit. How much do you have?'

'Millions,' said Henry.

Perfect Peter gasped.

'You do not,' said Peter. 'Do you?'

Henry shook his bank. A thin rattle came from within.

'That doesn't sound like millions,' said Peter.

'That's 'cause five pound notes don't rattle, stupid,' said Henry.

'Mum! Henry called me stupid,' shrieked Peter.

'Stop being horrid, Henry!' shouted Mum.

Horrid Henry gave the lid of his bank a final yank and spilled the contents on to the floor.

A single, solitary five pence coin rolled out.

Henry's jaw dropped. He grabbed the bank and fumbled around inside. It was empty.

'I've been robbed!' howled Horrid Henry. 'Where's my money? Who stole my money?'

Mum ran into the room.

'What's all this fuss?'

'Peter stole my money!' screamed Henry. He glared at his brother. 'Just wait until I get my hands on you, you little thief, I'll —'

'No one stole your money, Henry,' said Mum. 'You've spent it all on sweets and comics.'

'I have not!' shrieked Henry.

Mum pointed at the enormous pile of comics and sweet wrappers littering the floor of Henry's bedroom.

'What's all that then?' asked Mum.

Horrid Henry stopped shrieking. It was true. He *had* spent all his pocket money on comics and sweets. He just hadn't noticed.

'It's not fair!' he screamed.

'I saved all *my* pocket money, Mum,' said Perfect Peter. 'After all, a penny saved is a penny earned.'

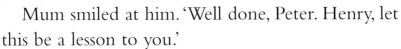

Mum smiled at him. 'Well done, Peter. Henry, let this be a lesson to you.'

'I can't wait to buy my nature kit,' said Perfect Peter. 'You should have saved your money like I did, instead of wasting it, Henry.'

Henry growled and sprang at Peter. He was an Indian warrior scalping a settler.

'YOWWWW!' squealed Peter.

'Henry! Stop it!' shouted Mum. 'Say sorry to Peter.'

'I'm not sorry!' screamed Henry. 'I want my money!'

'Any more nonsense from you, young man, and we won't be going to Toy Heaven,' said Mum.

Henry scowled.

'I don't care,' he muttered. What was the point of going to Toy Heaven if he couldn't buy any toys?

Horrid Henry lay on his bedroom floor kicking sweet wrappers. That Dungeon Drink kit cost £4.99. He had to get some money by tomorrow. The question was, how?

He could steal Peter's money. That was tempting, as he knew the secret place in Peter's cello case where Peter hid his bank. Wouldn't that be fun when Peter discovered his money was gone? Henry smiled.

On second thoughts, perhaps not. Mum and Dad would be sure to suspect Henry, especially if he suddenly had money and Peter didn't.

He could sell some of his comics to Moody Margaret.

'No!' shrieked Henry, clutching his comics to his chest. Not his precious comics. There *had* to be another way.

Then Henry had a wonderful, spectacular idea. It was so superb that he did a wild war dance for joy. That Dungeon Drink kit was as good as his. And, better still, Peter would give him all the money he needed. Henry chortled. This would be as easy as taking sweets from a baby . . . and a lot more fun.

Horrid Henry strolled down the hall to Peter's room. Peter was having a meeting of the Best Boys Club (motto: Can I help?) with his friends Tidy Ted, Spotless Sam and Goody-Goody Gordon. What luck. More money for him. Henry smiled as he put his ear to the keyhole and listened to them discussing their good deeds.

'I helped an old lady cross the road *and* I ate all my vegetables,' said Perfect Peter.

'I kept my room tidy all week,' said Tidy Ted.

'I scrubbed the bath without being asked,' said Spotless Sam.

'I never once forgot to say please and thank you,' said Goody-Goody Gordon.

Henry pushed past the barricades and burst into Peter's room.

'Password!' screeched Perfect Peter.

'Vitamins,' said Horrid Henry.

'How did you know?' said Tidy Ted, staring open-mouthed at Henry.

'Never you mind,' said Henry, who was not a master spy for nothing. 'I don't suppose any of you know about Fangmanglers?'

The boys looked at one another.

'What are they?' asked Spotless Sam.

'Only the slimiest, scariest, most horrible and frightening monsters in the whole world,' said Henry. 'And I know where to find one.'

'Where?' said Goody-Goody Gordon.

'I'm not going to tell you,' said Horrid Henry.

'Oh please!' said Spotless Sam.

Henry shook his head and lowered his voice.

'Fangmanglers only come out at night,' whispered
Henry. 'They slip into the shadows then sneak out and
. . . BITE YOU!' he suddenly shrieked.

The Best Boys Club members gasped with fright.

'I'm not scared,' said Peter. 'And I've never heard of
a Fangmangler.'

'That's because you're too young,' said Henry.
'Grown-ups don't tell you about them because they
don't want to scare you.'

'I want to see it,' said Tidy Ted.

'Me too,' said Spotless Sam and Goody-Goody Gordon.

Peter hesitated for a moment.

'Is this a trick, Henry?'

'Of course not,' said Henry. 'And just for that I won't let you come.'

'Oh please, Henry,' said Peter.

Henry paused.

'All right,' he said. 'We'll meet in the back garden after dark. But it will cost you two pounds each.'

'Two pounds!' they squealed.

'Do you want to see a Fangmangler or don't you?'

Perfect Peter exchanged a look with his friends.

They all nodded.

'Good,' said Horrid Henry. 'See you at six o'clock. And don't forget to bring your money.'

Tee hee, chortled Henry silently. Eight pounds! He could get a Dungeon Drink kit *and* a Grisly Ghoul Grub box at this rate.

Loud screams came from next-door's garden.

'Give me back my spade!' came Moody Margaret's bossy tones.

'You're so mean, Margaret,' squealed Sour Susan's sulky voice. 'Well, I won't. It's my turn to dig with it now.'

WHACK! THWACK!

'WAAAAAAA!'

Eight pounds is nice, thought Horrid Henry, but twelve is even nicer.

'What's going on?' asked Horrid Henry, smirking as he leapt over the wall.

'Go away, Henry!' shouted Moody Margaret.

'Yeah, Henry,' echoed Sour Susan, wiping away her tears. 'We don't want you.'

'All right,' said Henry. 'Then I won't tell you about the Fangmangler I've found.'

'We don't want to know about it,' said Margaret, turning her back on him.

'That's right,' said Susan.

'Well then, don't blame me when the Fangmangler sneaks over the wall and rips you to pieces and chews up your guts,' said Horrid Henry. He turned to go.

The girls looked at one another.

'Wait,' ordered Margaret.

'Yeah?' said Henry.

'You don't scare me,' said Margaret.

'Prove it then,' said Henry.

'How?' said Margaret.

'Be in my garden at six o'clock tonight and I'll show you the Fangmangler. But it will cost you two pounds each.'

'Forget it,' said Margaret. 'Come on, Susan.'

'OK,' said Henry quickly. 'A pound each.'

'No,' said Margaret.

'And your money back if the Fangmangler doesn't scare you,' said Henry.

Moody Margaret smiled.

'It's a deal,' she said.

When the coast was clear, Horrid Henry crept into the bushes and hid a bag containing his supplies: an old, torn T-shirt, some filthy trousers and a jumbo-sized bottle of ketchup. Then he sneaked back into the house and waited for dark.

'Thank you, thank you, thank you, thank you,' said Horrid Henry, collecting two pounds from each member of the Best Boys Club. Henry placed the money carefully in his skeleton bank. Boy, was he rich!

Moody Margaret and Sour Susan handed over a pound each.

'Remember, Henry, we get our money back if we aren't scared,' hissed Moody Margaret.

'Shut up, Margaret,' said Henry. 'I'm risking my life

and all you can think about is money. Now everyone, wait here, don't move and don't talk,' he whispered. 'We have to surprise the Fangmangler. If not . . .' Henry paused and drew his fingers across his throat.

'I'm a goner. I'm going off now to hunt for the monster. When I find him, and if it's safe, I'll whistle twice. Then everyone come, as quietly as you can. But be careful!'

Henry disappeared into the black darkness of the garden.

For a long, long moment there was silence.

'This is stupid,' said Moody Margaret.

Suddenly, a low, moaning growl echoed through the moonless night.

'What was that?' said Spotless Sam nervously.

'Henry? Are you all right, Henry?' squeaked Perfect Peter.

The low moaning growl turned into a snarl.

THRASH! CRASH!

'HELP! HELP! THE FANGMANGLER'S AFTER ME! RUN FOR YOUR LIVES!' screamed Horrid Henry, smashing through the bushes. His T-shirt and trousers were torn. There was blood everywhere.

The Best Boys Club screamed and ran.

Sour Susan screamed and ran.

Moody Margaret screamed and ran.

Horrid Henry screamed and . . . stopped.

He waited until he was alone. Then Horrid Henry wiped some ketchup from his face, clutched his bank and did a war dance round the garden, whooping with joy.

'Money! Money! Money! Money! Money!' he squealed, leaping and stomping. He danced and he pranced, he twirled and he whirled. He was so busy dancing and cackling he didn't notice a shadowy shape slip into the garden behind him.

'Money! Money! Money! Mine! Mine –' he broke off. What was that noise? Horrid Henry's throat tightened.

Nah, he thought. It's nothing.

Then suddenly a dark shape leapt out of the bushes and let out a thunderous roar.

Horrid Henry shrieked with terror. He dropped his money and ran for his life. The Thing scooped up his bank and slithered over the wall.

Horrid Henry did not stop running until he was safely in his room with the door shut tight and barricaded. His heart pounded.

There really is a Fangmangler, he thought, trembling. And now it's after *me.*

Horrid Henry hardly slept a wink. He started awake at every squeak and creak. He shook and he shrieked. Henry had such a bad night that he slept in quite late the next morning, tossing and turning.

FIZZ! POP! GURGLE! BANG!

Henry jerked awake. What was that? He peeked his head out from under the duvet and listened.

FIZZ! POP! GURGLE! BANG!

Those fizzing and popping noises seemed to be coming from next door.

Henry ran to the window and pulled open the curtains. There was Moody Margaret sitting beside a large Toy Heaven bag. In front of her was . . .

a Dungeon Drink kit. She saw him, smiled, and raised a glass of bubbling black liquid.

'Want a Fangmangler drink, Henry?' asked Margaret sweetly.

❀ Dear Mum and Dad ❀

In case you forgot, it's my
birthday in 2 months
and 13 days.
I want lots of toys.
And ^LOTS of money is always good

Henry

P.s.   Vests, socks and books
       are NOT presents.

Dear Henry's Parents,
I am sorry to tell you that
today Henry poked Brian,
pinched Gurinder, made
rude faces, broke Margaret's
pencil, ate sweets in class,
failed his maths test and
did not hand in his
homework.
Please come in and see me
IMMEDIATELY!
Boudicca Battle-Axe

Sam
Would like to
.....Peter
To his Birthda
At
Our Town Me

Henry
Come to my
BIRTHDAY PARTY
At Lazer Zap
Toby

Stinky

Ugly! Pongy! Nappie-face! TOAD!

HORRID HENRY
TRICKS THE
TOOTH FAIRY

'It's not fair!' shrieked Horrid Henry. He trampled on Dad's new flower-bed, squashing the pansies. 'It's just not fair!'

Moody Margaret had lost two teeth. Sour Susan had lost three. Clever Clare lost two in one day. Rude Ralph had lost four, two top and two bottom, and could spit to the blackboard from his desk. Greedy Graham's teeth were pouring out. Even Weepy William had lost one – and that was ages ago.

Every day someone swaggered into school showing off a big black toothy gap and waving 50p or even a pound that the Tooth Fairy had brought. Everyone, that is, but Henry.

'It's not fair!' shouted Henry again. He yanked on his teeth. He pulled, he pushed, he tweaked, and he tugged.

They would not budge.

His teeth were superglued to his gums.

'Why me?' moaned Henry, stomping on the petunias. 'Why am I the only one who hasn't lost a tooth?'

Horrid Henry sat in his fort and scowled. He was sick and tired of other kids flaunting their ugly wobbly teeth and disgusting holes in their gums. The next person who so much as mentioned the word 'tooth' had better watch out.

'HENRY!' shouted a squeaky little voice. 'Where are you?'

Horrid Henry hid behind the branches.

'I know you're in the fort, Henry,' said Perfect Peter.

'Go away!' said Henry.

'Look, Henry,' said Peter. 'I've got something wonderful to show you.'

Henry scowled. 'What?'

'You have to see it,' said Peter.

Peter never had anything good to show. His idea of something wonderful was a new stamp, or a book about plants, or a gold star from his teacher saying how perfect he'd been. Still . . .

Henry crawled out.

'This had better be good,' he said. 'Or you're in big trouble.'

Peter held out his fist and opened it.

There was something small and white in Peter's hand. It looked like . . . no, it couldn't be.

Henry stared at Peter. Peter smiled as wide as he could. Henry's jaw dropped. This was impossible. His eyes must be playing tricks on him.

Henry blinked. Then he blinked again.

His eyes were not playing tricks. Perfect Peter, his *younger* brother, had a black gap at the bottom of his mouth where a tooth had been.

Henry grabbed Peter. 'You've coloured in your tooth with black crayon, you faker.'

'Have not!' shrieked Peter. 'It fell out. See.'

Peter proudly poked his finger through the hole in his mouth.

It was true. Perfect Peter had lost a tooth. Henry felt as if a fist had slammed into his stomach.

'Told you,' said Peter. He smiled again at Henry.

Henry could not bear to look at Peter's gappy teeth a second longer. This was the worst thing that had ever happened to him.

'I hate you!' shrieked Henry. He was a volcano pouring hot molten lava on to the puny human foolish enough to get in his way.

'AAAAGGGGHHHH!' screeched Peter, dropping the tooth.

Henry grabbed it.

'OWWWW!' yelped Peter. 'Give me back my tooth!'

'Stop being horrid, Henry!' shouted Mum.

Henry dangled the tooth in front of Peter.

'Nah nah ne nah nah,' jeered Henry.

Peter burst into tears.

'Give me back my tooth!' screamed Peter.

Mum ran into the garden.

'Give Peter his tooth this minute,' said Mum.

'No,' said Henry.

Mum looked fierce. She put out her hand. 'Give it to me right now.'

Henry dropped the tooth on the ground.

'There,' said Horrid Henry.

'That's it, Henry,' said Mum. 'No pudding tonight.'

Henry was too miserable to care.

Peter scooped up his tooth. 'Look, Mum,' said Peter.

'My big boy!' said Mum, giving him a hug. 'How wonderful.'

'I'm going to use my money from the Tooth Fairy to buy some stamps for my collection,' said Peter.

'What a good idea,' said Mum.

Henry stuck out his tongue.

'Henry's sticking out his tongue at me,' said Peter.

'Stop it, Henry,' said Mum. 'Peter, keep that tooth safe for the Tooth Fairy.'

'I will,' said Peter. He closed his fist tightly round the tooth.

Henry sat in his fort. If a tooth wouldn't fall out, he would have to help it. But what to do? He could take a hammer and smash one out. Or he could tie string round a tooth, tie the string round a door handle and slam the door. Eek! Henry grabbed his jaw.

On second thoughts, perhaps not. Maybe there was

a less painful way of losing a tooth. What was it the dentist always said? Eat too many sweets and your teeth will fall out?

Horrid Henry sneaked into the kitchen. He looked to the right. He looked to the left. No one was there. From the sitting room came the screechy scratchy sound of Peter practising his cello.

Henry dashed to the cupboard where Mum kept the sweet jar. Sweet day was Saturday, and today was Thursday. Two whole days before he got into trouble.

Henry stuffed as many sticky sweets into his mouth as fast as he could.

Chomp Chomp Chomp Chomp.

Chomp Chew Chomp Chew.

Chompa Chew

Chompa Chew.

Chompa ...
Chompa ...
C h o m p a ...

C h o m p a ...

C h e w

Henry's jaw started to slow down. He put the last  sticky toffee in his mouth and forced his teeth to move up and down.

Henry started to feel sick. His teeth felt even sicker. He wiggled them hopefully. After all that sugar one was sure to fall out. He could see all the comics he would buy with his pound already.

Henry wiggled his teeth again. And again.

Nothing moved.

Rats, thought Henry. His mouth hurt. His gums hurt. His tummy hurt. What did a boy have to do to get a tooth?

Then Henry had a wonderful, spectacular idea. It was so wonderful that he hugged himself. Why should Peter get a pound from the Tooth Fairy? Henry would get that pound, not him. And how? Simple. He would trick the Tooth Fairy.

The house was quiet. Henry tiptoed into Peter's room. There was Peter, sound asleep, a big smile on his face. Henry sneaked his hand under Peter's pillow and stole the tooth.

Tee hee, thought Henry. He tiptoed out of Peter's room and bumped into Mum.

'AAAAGGGHH!' shrieked Henry.

'AAAAGGGHH!' shrieked Mum.

'You scared me,' said Henry.

'What are you doing?' said Mum.

'Nothing,' said Henry. 'I thought I heard a noise in Peter's room and went to check.'

Mum looked at Henry. Henry tried to look sweet.

'Go back to bed, Henry,' said Mum.

Henry scampered to his room and put the tooth under his pillow. Phew. That was a close call. Henry smiled. Wouldn't that crybaby Peter be furious the next morning when he found no tooth and no money?

Henry woke up and felt under his pillow. The tooth was gone. Hooray, thought Henry. Now for the money.

Henry searched under the pillow.

Henry searched on top of the pillow.

He searched under the covers, under Teddy, under the bed, everywhere. There was no money.

Henry heard Peter's footsteps pounding down the hall.

'Mum, Dad, look,' said Peter. 'A whole pound from the Tooth Fairy!'

'Great!' said Mum.

'Wonderful!' said Dad.

What?! thought Henry.

'Shall I share it with you, Mum?' said Peter.

'Thank you, darling Peter, but no thanks,' said Mum. 'It's for you.'

'I'll have it,' said Henry. 'There are loads of comics I want to buy. And some —'

'No,' said Peter. 'It's mine. Get your own tooth.'

Henry stared at his brother. Peter would never have dared to speak to him like that before.

Horrid Henry pretended he was a pirate captain pushing a prisoner off the plank.

'OWWW!' shrieked Peter.

'Don't be horrid, Henry,' said Dad.

Henry decided to change the subject fast.

'Mum,' said Henry. 'How does the Tooth Fairy *know* who's lost a tooth?'

'She looks under the pillow,' said Mum.

'But how does she know whose pillow to look under?'

'She just does,' said Mum. 'By magic.'

'But how?' said Henry.

'She sees the gap between your teeth,' said Mum.

Aha, thought Henry. That's where he'd gone wrong.

That night Henry cut out a small piece of black paper, wet it, and covered over his two bottom teeth. He smiled at himself in the mirror. Perfect, thought Henry. He smiled again.

Then Henry stuck a pair of Dracula teeth under his pillow. He tied a string round the biggest tooth, and tied the string to his finger. When the Tooth Fairy came, the string would pull on his finger and wake him up.

All right, Tooth Fairy, thought Henry. You think you're so smart. Find your way out of this one.

The next morning was Saturday. Henry woke up and felt under his pillow. The string was still attached to his finger, but the Dracula teeth were gone. In their place was something small and round . . .

'My pound coin!' crowed Henry. He grabbed it.

The pound coin was plastic.

There must be some mistake, thought Henry. He checked under the pillow again. But all he found was a folded piece of bright blue paper, covered in stars.

Henry opened it. There, in tiny letters, he read:

Nice try Henry

The Tooth Fairy

'Rats,' said Henry.

From downstairs came the sound of Mum shouting.

'Henry! Get down here this minute!'

'What now?' muttered Henry, heaving his heavy bones out of bed.

'Yeah?' said Henry.

Mum help up an empty jar.

'Well?' said Mum.

Henry had forgotten all about the sweets.

'It wasn't me,' said Henry automatically. 'We must have mice.'

'No sweets for a month,' said Mum. 'You'll eat apples instead. You can start right now.'

Ugh. Apples. Henry hated all fruits and vegetables, but apples were the worst.

'Oh no,' said Henry.

'Oh yes,' said Mum. 'Right now.'

Henry took the apple and bit off the teeniest, tiniest piece he could.

CRUNCH.   CRACK.

Henry choked. Then he swallowed, gasping and spluttering.

His mouth felt funny. Henry poked around with his tongue and felt a space.

He shoved his fingers in his mouth, then ran to the mirror.

His tooth was gone.
He'd swallowed it.
'It's not fair!' shrieked Horrid Henry.

Dear Tooth Fairy
Dont you think it's time to start bringing £2 coins?
Yor friend
Henry

Peter's Room

Henry's Room

Mum and Dad

Just to remind you, it's my birthday in 1 month and 7 days. I need a Rapper Zapper lunchbox! And a Terminater Gladiator Sord and Shield! And Siren Trainers with the flashing red lights! And the Intergalactic Samurai Gurillas which launch real Stink bombs

~~If you don't buy them for me~~
~~You'll be very sorry~~
~~If you don't buy them for me~~
~~I'll be sorry~~

Buy them or else. Henry

HORRID HENRY GETS RICH QUICK

Horrid Henry loved money. He loved counting money. He loved holding money. He loved spending money. There was only one problem. Horrid Henry never had any money.

He sat on his bedroom floor and rattled his empty skeleton bank. How his mean parents expected him to get by on 50p a week pocket money he would never know. It was so unfair! Why should they have all the money when there were so many things *he* needed? Comic books. Whopper chocolate bars. A new football. More knights for his castle. Horrid Henry looked round his room, scowling. True, his shelves were filled with toys, but nothing he still wanted to play with.

'MUM!' screamed Henry.

'Stop shouting, Henry,' shouted Mum. 'If you have something to say come downstairs and say it.'

'I need more pocket money,' said Henry. 'Ralph gets a pound a week.'

'Different children get different amounts,' said Mum. 'I think 50p a week is perfectly adequate.'

'Well I don't,' said Henry.

'I'm very happy with *my* pocket money, Mum,' said Perfect Peter. 'I always save loads from my 30p. After all, if you look after the pennies the pounds will look after themselves.'

'Quite right, Peter,' said Mum, smiling.

Henry walked slowly past Peter. When Mum wasn't looking he reached out and grabbed him. He was a giant crab crushing a prawn in its claws.

'OWWW!' wailed Peter. 'Henry pinched me!'

'I did not,' said Henry.

'No pocket money for a week, Henry,' said Mum.

'That's not fair!' howled Henry. 'I need money!'

'You'll just have to save more,' said Mum.

'No!' shouted Henry. He hated saving money.

'Then you'll have to find a way to earn some,' said Mum.

Earn? Earn money? Suddenly Henry had a brilliant, fantastic idea.

'Mum, can I set up a stall and sell some stuff I don't want?'

'Like what?' said Mum.

'You know, old toys, comics, games, things I don't use any more,' said Henry.

Mum hesitated for a moment. She couldn't think of anything wrong with selling off old junk.

'All right,' said Mum.

'Can I help, Henry?' said Peter.

'No way,' said Henry.

'Oh please,' said Peter.

'Stop being horrid, Henry, and let Peter help you,' said Mum, 'or no stall.'

'OK,' said Henry, scowling, 'you can make the For Sale signs.'

Horrid Henry ran to his bedroom and piled his unwanted jumble into a box. He cleared his shelves of books, his wardrobe of party clothes, and his toybox of puzzles with pieces missing.

Then Horrid Henry paused. To make big money he definitely needed a few more valuable items. Now, where could he find some?

Henry crept into Peter's room. He could sell Peter's stamp collection, or his nature kit. Nah, thought Henry, no one would want that boring stuff.

Then Henry glanced inside Mum and Dad's room. It was packed with rich pickings. Henry sauntered over to Mum's dressing table. Look at all that perfume, thought Henry, she wouldn't miss one bottle. He chose a large crystal bottle with a swan-shaped stopper

and packed it in the box. Now, what other jumble could he find?

Aha! There was Dad's tennis racquet. Dad never played tennis. That racquet was just lying there collecting dust when it could go to a much better home.

Perfect, thought Henry, adding the racquet to his collection. Then he staggered out to the pavement to set up the display.

Horrid Henry surveyed his stall. It was piled high with great bargains. He should make a fortune.

'But Henry,' said Peter, looking up from drawing a sign, 'that's Dad's tennis racquet. Are you sure he wants you to sell it?'

'Of course I'm sure, stupid,' snapped Henry. If only he could get rid of his horrible brother, wouldn't life be perfect.

Then Horrid Henry looked at Peter. What was it

the Romans did with their leftover captives? Hmmn, he thought. He looked again. Hmmmn, he thought.

'Peter,' said Henry sweetly, 'would you like to earn some money?'

'Oh yes!' said Peter. 'How?'

'We could sell you as a slave.'

Perfect Peter thought for a moment.

'How much would I get?'

'10p,' said Henry.

'Wow,' said Peter. 'That means I'll have £6.47 in my piggybank. Can I wear a For Sale sign?'

'Certainly,' said Horrid Henry. He scribbled: For Sale £5, then placed the sign round Peter's neck.

'Now look smart,' said Henry. 'I see some customers coming.'

'What's going on?' said Moody Margaret.

'Yeah, Henry, what are you doing?' said Sour Susan.

'I'm having a jumble sale,' said Henry. 'Lots of

72

bargains. All the money raised will go to a very good cause.'

'What's that?' said Susan.

'Children in Need,' said Henry. I am a child and I'm certainly in need so that's true, he thought.

Moody Margaret picked up a punctured football.

'Bargain? This is just a lot of old junk.'

'No it isn't,' said Henry. 'Look. Puzzles, books, perfume, stuffed toys, *and* a slave.'

Moody Margaret looked up.

'I could use a good slave,' said Margaret. 'I'll give you 25p for him.'

'25p for an excellent slave? He's worth at least £1.50.'

'Make a muscle, slave,' said Moody Margaret.

Perfect Peter made a muscle.

'Hmmn,' said Margaret. '50p is my final offer.'

'Done,' said Horrid Henry. Why had he never thought of selling Peter before?

'How come I get 10p when I cost 50p?' said Peter.

'Shopkeeper's expenses,' said Henry. 'Now run along with your new owner.'

Business was brisk.

Rude Ralph bought some football cards.

Sour Susan bought Best Bear and Mum's perfume.

Beefy Bert bought a racing car with three wheels.

Then Aerobic Al jogged by.

'Cool racquet,' he said, picking up Dad's racquet and giving it a few swings. 'How much?'

'£10,' said Henry.

'I'll give you £2,' said Al.

£2! That was more money than Horrid Henry had ever had in his life! He was rich!

'Done,' said Henry.

Horrid Henry sat in the sitting room gazing happily at his stacks of money. £3.12! Boy, would that buy a lot of chocolate! Mum came into the room.

'Henry, have you seen my new perfume? You know, the one with the swan on top.'

'No,' said Henry. Yikes, he never thought she would notice.

'And where's Peter?' said Mum. 'I thought he was playing with you.'

'He's gone,' said Henry.

Mum stared at him.

'What do you mean, gone?'

'Gone,' said Henry, popping a crisp into his mouth. 'I sold him.'

'You did what?' whispered Mum. Her face was pale.

'You said I could sell anything I didn't want, and I certainly didn't want Peter, so I sold him to Margaret.'

Mum's jaw dropped.

'You go straight over to Margaret's and buy him back!' screamed Mum. 'You horrid boy! Selling your own brother!'

'But I don't want him back,' said Henry.

'No ifs or buts, Henry!' screeched Mum. 'You just get your brother back.'

'I can't afford to buy him,' said Horrid Henry. 'If you want him back you should pay for him.'

'HENRY!' bellowed Mum.

'All right,' grumbled Henry, getting to his feet. He sighed. What a waste of good money, he thought, climbing over the wall into Margaret's garden.

Margaret was lying by the paddling pool.

'SLAVE!' she ordered. 'I'm hot! Fan me!'

Perfect Peter came out of her house carrying a large fan.

He started to wave it in Moody Margaret's direction.

'Faster, slave!' said Margaret.

Peter fanned faster.

'Slower, slave!' said Margaret.

Peter fanned slower.

'Slave! A cool drink, and make it snappy!' ordered Margaret.

Horrid Henry followed Peter back into the kitchen.

'Henry!' squeaked Peter. 'Have you come to rescue me?'

'No,' said Henry.

'Please,' said Peter. 'I'll do anything. You can have the 10p.'

The cash register in Henry's head started to whirl.

'Not enough,' said Henry.

'I'll give you 50p. I'll give you £1. I'll give you £2,' said Peter. 'She's horrible. She's even worse than you.'

'Right, you can stay here for ever,' said Henry.

'Sorry, Henry,' said Perfect Peter. 'You're the best brother in the world. I'll give you all my money.'

Horrid Henry looked as if he were considering this offer.

'All right, wait here,' said Henry. 'I'll see what I can do.'

'Thank you, Henry,' said Peter.

Horrid Henry went back into the garden.

'Where's my drink?' said Margaret.

'My mum says I have to have Peter back,' said Henry.

Moody Margaret gazed at him.

'Oh yeah?'

'Yeah,' said Henry.

'Well I don't want to sell him,' said Margaret. 'I paid good money for him.'

Henry had hoped she'd forgotten that.

'OK, here's the 50p,' he said.

Moody Margaret lay back and closed her eyes.

'I haven't spent all this time and effort training him just to get my money back,' she said. 'He's worth at least £10 now.'

Slowly Henry stuck his hand back into his pocket.

'75p and that's my final offer.'

Moody Margaret knew a good deal when she was offered one.

'OK,' she said. 'Give me my money.'

Reluctantly, Henry paid her. But that still leaves over £2, thought Henry, so I'm well ahead.

Then he went in to fetch Peter.

'You cost me £6,' he said.

'Thank you, Henry,' said Peter. 'I'll pay you as soon as we get home.'

Yippee! thought Horrid Henry. I'm super rich! The world is mine!

Clink, clank, clink, went Henry's heavy pockets as Henry did his money dance.

 **'CLINK, CLANK, CLINK, I'm rich, I'm rich, I'm rich, I'm rich as I can be,'**

sang Henry.

Spend, spend, spend would be his motto from now on.

'Hello everybody,' called Dad, coming through the front door. 'What a lovely afternoon! Anyone for tennis?'

Horrid Henry's Prized Possessions

Dear Father Chrismas

I want loads of money
and a ROBOMATIC
SUPERSONIC SPACE
HOWLER with all the
attachments
Mum and Dad want me to
have one too.

Henry

P.S. Peter has been horrible
all year and deserves **NO**
presents
Please give his to me

I'm telling on you.

Tattle-tale

HORRID HENRY'S
CHORES

The weekend! The lovely, lovely weekend. Sleeping in. Breakfast in his pyjamas. Morning TV. Afternoon TV. Evening TV. No school and no Miss Battle-Axe for two whole days.

In fact, there was only one bad thing about the weekend. Henry didn't even want to think about it. Maybe Mum would forget, he thought hopefully. Maybe today would be the day she didn't burst in and ruin everything.

Horrid Henry settled down in the comfy black chair and switched on his new favourite TV show, *Hog House*, where teenagers competed to see whose room was the most disgusting.

Henry couldn't wait till he was a terrible teen too. His bedroom would surely beat anything ever seen on *Hog House*.

'Eeeew,' squealed Horrid Henry happily, as Filthy Phil showed off what he kept under his bed.

'Yuck!' shrieked Horrid Henry, as Mouldy Myra yanked open her cupboard.

'Oooh, gross!' howled Horrid Henry, as Tornado Tariq showed why his family had moved out.

'And this week's winner for the most revolting room is –'

CLUNK
CLUNK
CLUNK

Mum clanked in. She was dragging her favourite instruments of torture: a hoover and a duster. Peter followed.

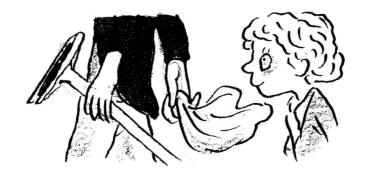

'Henry, turn off that horrid programme this minute,' said Mum. 'It's time to do your chores.'

'NO!' screamed Horrid Henry.

Was there a more hateful, horrible word in the world than chores? *Chores* was worse than *homework*. Worse than *vegetables*. Even worse than *injection*, *share*, and *bedtime*. When he was King no child would ever have to do chores. Any parent who so much as whispered the word *chores* would get catapulted over the battlements into the piranha-infested moat.

'You can start by picking up your dirty socks from the floor,' said Mum.

Pick up a sock? Pick up a sock? Was there no end to Mum's meanness? Who cared if he had a few old socks scattered around the place?

'I can't believe you're making me do this!' screamed Henry. He glared at Mum. Then he glared at his crumpled socks. The socks were miles away from the sofa. He'd pick them up later. Much later.

'Henry, your turn to hoover the sitting room,' said Mum. 'Peter, your turn to dust.'

'No!' howled Horrid Henry. 'I'm allergic to hoovers.'

Mum ignored him.

'Then empty the bins and put the dirty clothes into the washing machine. And make sure you separate the whites from the coloureds.'

Henry didn't move.

'It will only take fifteen minutes,' said Mum.

'It's not fair!' wailed Henry. 'I hoovered last week.'

'No you didn't, I did,' said Peter.

'I did!' screamed Henry. 'Liar!'

'Liar!'

'Can't I do it later?' said Horrid Henry. Later had such a happy way of turning into never.

'N-O spells no,' said Mum.

Peter started dusting the TV.

'Stop it!' said Henry. 'I'm watching.'

'I'm dusting,' said Peter.

86

'Out of my way, worm,' hissed Horrid Henry.

Mum marched over and switched off the TV. 'No TV until you do your chores, Henry. Everyone has to pitch in and help in this family.'

Horrid Henry was outraged. Why should he help around the house? That was his lazy parents' job. Didn't he work hard enough already, heaving his heavy bones to school every day?

And all the schoolwork he did! It was amazing, thought Horrid Henry, as he lay kicking and screaming on the sofa, that he was still alive.

'I WON'T! I'M NOT YOUR SLAVE!'

'Henry, it's not fair if Mum and Dad do *all* the housework,' said Perfect Peter.

That seemed fair to Henry.

'Quite right, Peter,' said Mum, beaming. 'What a lovely thoughtful boy you are.'

'Shut up, Peter!' screamed Henry.

'Don't be horrid, Henry!' screamed Mum.

'No TV and no pocket money until you do your chores,' said Dad, running in.

Henry stopped screaming.

No pocket money! No TV!

'I don't need any pocket money,' shrieked Henry.

'Fine,' said Mum.

Wait, what was he saying?

Of course he needed pocket money. How else would he buy sweets? And he'd die if he couldn't watch TV.

'I'm calling the police,' said Horrid Henry. 'They'll come and arrest you for child cruelty.'

'Finished!' sang out Perfect Peter. 'I've done all *my* chores,' he added, 'can I have my pocket money please?'

'Of course you can,' said Mum. She handed Peter a shiny 50p piece.

Horrid Henry glared at Peter. Could that ugly toad get any uglier?

'All right,' snarled Henry. 'I'll hoover. And out of my way, frog face, or I'll hoover you up.'

'Mum!' wailed Peter. 'Henry's trying to hoover me.'

'Just do your chores, Henry,' said Mum. She felt tired.

'You could have done *all* your chores in the time you've spent arguing,' said Dad. He felt tired, too.

Henry slammed the sitting room door behind his mean, horrible parents. He looked at the hoover with loathing. Why didn't that stupid machine just hoover by itself? A robot hoover, that's what he needed.

Henry switched it on.

VROOM! VROOM!

'Hoover, hoover!' ordered Henry.

The hoover did not move.

'Go on, hoover, you can do it,' said Henry.

VROOM! VROOM!

Still the hoover didn't move.

What a lot of noise that stupid machine makes, thought Henry. I bet you can hear it all over the house.

And then suddenly Horrid Henry had a brilliant, spectacular idea. Why had he never thought of it before? He'd ask to hoover every week.

Henry dragged the hoover over to the sitting room door and left it roaring there. Then he flopped on the sofa and switched on the TV. Great, *Hog House* hadn't finished!

Mum and Dad listened to the hoover blaring from the sitting room. Goodness, Henry was working hard. They were amazed.

'Isn't Henry doing a good job,' said Mum.

'He's been working over thirty minutes non-stop,' said Dad.

'Finally, he's being responsible,' said Mum.

'At last,' said Dad.

'Go Tariq!' cheered Henry, as Tornado Tariq blew into his parents' tidy bedroom. Ha ha ha, chortled Henry, what a shock those parents would get.

'Stay tuned for the Filthy Final between Tariq and Myra, coming up in three minutes!' said the presenter, Dirty Dirk.

Footsteps. Yikes, someone was coming.

Oh no.

Henry sprang from the sofa, turned off the telly and grabbed the hoover.

Mum walked in.

Horrid Henry began to pant.

'I've worked so hard, Mum,' gasped Henry. 'Please can I stop now?'

Mum stared at the dustballs covering the carpet.

'But Henry,' said Mum. 'There's still dust everywhere.'

'I can't help it,' said Henry. 'I did my best.'

'All right, Henry,' said Mum, sighing.

YES! thought Horrid Henry.

'But remember, no TV until you've emptied the bins and separated the laundry.'

'I know, I know,' muttered Henry, running up the stairs. If he finished his chores in the next two minutes, he'd be in time for the *Hog House* final!

Right. Mum said to empty the bins. She didn't say into what, just that the bins had to be empty.

It was the work of a few moments to tip all the wastepaper baskets onto the floor.

That's done, thought Horrid Henry, racing down the stairs. Now that stupid laundry. When he was a billionaire computer game tester, he'd never wash his clothes. He'd just buy new ones.

Horrid Henry glared at the dirty clothes piled on the floor in front of the washing machine. It would take him hours to separate the whites from the coloureds. What a waste of valuable time, thought Henry. Mum and Dad just made him do it to be mean. What difference could it make to wash a red sweatshirt with a white sheet? None.

Horrid Henry shoved all the clothes into the washing machine and slammed the door.

Free at last.

'Done!' shrieked Horrid Henry.

Wow, what a brilliant *Hog House* that was, thought Horrid Henry, jingling his pocket money. He wandered past the washing machine. Strange, he didn't remember all those pink clothes swirling around. Since when did his family have pink sheets and pink towels?

Since he'd washed a red sweatshirt with the whites. Uh oh.

Mum would be furious. Dad would be furious. His punishment would be terrible. Hide! thought Horrid Henry.

Dad stared at his newly pink underpants, shirts, and vests.

Mum stared at her best white skirt, now her worst pink one.

Henry stared at the floor. This time there was no escape.

'Maybe we're asking too much of you,' said Dad, gazing at the trail of rubbish lying round the house.

'You're just not responsible enough,' said Mum.

'Too clumsy,' said Dad.

'Too young,' said Mum.

'Maybe it's easier if we do the chores ourselves,' said Dad.

'Maybe it is,' said Mum.

Horrid Henry could hardly believe his ears. No more chores? Because he was so bad at doing them?

'Yippee!' squealed Henry.

'On the other hand, maybe not,' said Dad, glaring. 'We'll see how well you do your chores next week.'

'OK,' said Horrid Henry agreeably.

He had the feeling his chore-doing skills wouldn't be improving.

Horrid Henry's Chores

CHORES

	week 1	week 2	week 3	week 4
Hoover sitting room	~~Henry~~ **Peter**	Peter	~~Henry~~ **Peter**	Peter
Dust	~~Henry~~ **Peter**	Peter	~~Henry~~ **Peter**	Peter
Empty bins	~~Henry~~ **Peter**	Peter	~~Henry~~ **Peter**	Peter
Wash Clothes	Peter	~~Henry~~ **Peter**	Peter	~~Henry~~ **Peter**

HORRiD HENRY
TRiCKS AND TREATS

Hallowe'en! Oh happy, happy day! Every year Horrid Henry could not believe it: an entire day devoted to stuffing your face with sweets and playing horrid tricks. Best of all, you were *supposed* to stuff your face and play horrid tricks. Whoopee!

Horrid Henry was armed and ready. He had loo roll. He had water pistols. He had shaving foam. Oh my, would he be playing tricks tonight. Anyone who didn't instantly hand over a fistful of sweets would get it with the foam. And woe betide any fool who gave him an apple. Horrid Henry knew how to treat rotten grown-ups like that.

His red and black devil costume lay ready on the bed, complete with evil mask, twinkling horns, trident, and whippy tail. He'd scare everyone wearing that.

'Heh heh heh,' said Horrid Henry, practising his evil laugh.

'Henry,' came a little voice outside his bedroom door, 'come and see my new costume.'

'No,' said Henry.

'Oh please, Henry,' said his younger brother, Perfect Peter.

'No,' said Henry. 'I'm busy.'

'You're just jealous because *my* costume is nicer than yours,' said Peter.

'Am not.'

'Are too.'

Come to think of it, what *was* Peter wearing? Last year he'd copied Henry's monster costume and ruined Henry's Hallowe'en. What if he were copying Henry's devil costume? That would be just like that horrible little copycat.

'All right, you can come in for two seconds,' said Henry.

A big, pink bouncy bunny bounded into Henry's room. It had little white bunny ears. It had a little white bunny tail. It had pink polka dots everywhere else. Horrid Henry groaned. What a stupid costume. Thank goodness *he* wasn't wearing it.

'Isn't it great?' said Perfect Peter.

'No,' said Henry. 'It's horrible.'

'You're just saying that to be mean, Henry,' said Peter, bouncing up and down. 'I can't wait to go trick-or-treating in it tonight.'

Oh no. Horrid Henry felt as if he'd been punched in the stomach. Henry would be expected to go out trick or treating – with Peter! He, Henry, would have to walk around with a pink polka dot bunny. Everyone would see him. The shame of it! Rude Ralph would never stop teasing him. Moody Margaret would call him a bunny wunny. How could he play tricks on people with a pink polka dot bunny following him everywhere? He was ruined. His name would be a joke.

'You can't wear that,' said Henry desperately.

'Yes I can,' said Peter.

'I won't let you,' said Henry.

Perfect Peter looked at Henry. 'You're just jealous.'

Grrr! Horrid Henry was about to tear that stupid costume off Peter when, suddenly, he had an idea.

It was painful.

It was humiliating.

But anything was better than having Peter prancing about in pink polka dots.

'Tell you what,' said Henry, 'just because I'm so nice I'll let you borrow my monster costume. You've always wanted to wear it.'

'NO!' said Peter. 'I want to be a bunny.'

'But you're supposed to be scary for Hallowe'en,' said Henry.

'I am scary,' said Peter. 'I'm going to bounce up to people and yell "boo".'

'I can make you really scary, Peter,' said Horrid Henry.

'How?' said Peter.

'Sit down and I'll show you.' Henry patted his desk chair.

'What are you going to do?' said Peter suspiciously. He took a step back.

'Nothing,' said Henry. 'I'm just trying to help you.'

Perfect Peter didn't move.

'How can I be scarier?' he said cautiously.

'I can give you a scary haircut,' said Henry.

Perfect Peter clutched his curls.

'But I like my hair,' he said feebly.

'This is Hallowe'en,' said Henry. 'Do you want to be scary or don't you?'

'Um, um, uh,' said Peter, as Henry pushed him down in the chair and got out the scissors.

'Not too much,' squealed Peter.

'Of course not,' said Horrid Henry. 'Just sit back and relax, I promise you'll love this.'

Horrid Henry twirled the scissors.

Snip! Snip! Snip! Snip! Snip!

Magnificent, thought Horrid Henry. He gazed proudly at his work. Maybe he should be a hairdresser when he grew up. Yes! Henry could see it now. Customers would queue for miles for one of Monsieur Henri's scary snips. Shame his genius was wasted on someone as yucky as Peter. Still . . .

'You look great, Peter,' said Henry. 'Really scary. Atomic Bunny. Go and have a look.'

Peter went over and looked in the mirror.

'AAAAAAAAAARGGGGGGGG!'

'Scared yourself, did you?' said Henry. 'That's great.'

'AAAAAAAAAARGGGGGGG!' howled Peter.

Mum ran into the room.

'AAAAAAAAAARGGGGGGG!' howled Mum.

'AAAAAAAAAARGGGGGGG!' howled Peter.

'Henry!' screeched Mum. 'What have you done! You horrid, horrid boy!'

What was left of Peter's hair stuck up in ragged tufts

all over his head. On one side was a big bald patch.

'I was just making him look scary,' protested Henry. 'He said I could.'

'Henry made me!' said Peter.

'My poor baby,' said Mum. She glared at Henry.

'No trick-or-treating for you,' said Mum. 'You'll stay here.'

Horrid Henry could hardly believe his ears. This was the worst thing that had ever happened to him.

'NO!' howled Henry. This was all Peter's fault.

'I hate you, Peter!' he screeched. Then he attacked. He was Medusa, coiling round her victim with her snaky hair.

'Aaaahh!' screeched Peter.

'Henry!' shouted Mum. 'Go to your room!'

Mum and Peter left the house to go trick-or-treating. Henry had screamed and sobbed and begged. He'd put on his devil costume, just in case his tears melted their stony hearts. But no. His mean, horrible parents wouldn't change their mind. Well, they'd be sorry. They'd all be sorry.

Dad came into the sitting room. He was holding a large shopping bag.

'Henry, I've got some work to finish so I'm going to let you hand out treats to any trick-or-treaters.'

Horrid Henry stopped plotting his revenge. Had Dad gone mad? Hand out treats? What kind of punishment was this?

Horrid Henry fought to keep a big smile off his face.

'Here's the Hallowe'en stuff, Henry,' said Dad. He handed Henry the heavy bag. 'But remember,' he added sternly, 'these treats are not for you: they're to give away.'

Yeah, right, thought Henry.

'OK, Dad,' he said as meekly as he could. 'Whatever you say.'

Dad went back to the kitchen. Now was his chance! Horrid Henry leapt on the bag. Wow, was it full! He'd grab all the good stuff, throw back anything yucky with lime or peppermint, and he'd have enough sweets to keep him going for at least a week!

Henry yanked open the bag. A terrible sight met his eyes. The bag was full of satsumas. And apples. And walnuts in their shells. No wonder his horrible parents had trusted him to be in charge of it.

Ding dong.

Slowly, Horrid Henry heaved his heavy bones to the door. There was his empty, useless trick-or-treat bag, sitting forlornly by the entrance.

Henry gave it a kick, then opened the door and glared.

'Whaddya want?' snapped Horrid Henry.

'Trick-or-treat,' whispered Weepy William. He was dressed as a pirate.

Horrid Henry held out the bag of horrors.

'Lucky dip!' he announced.

'Close your eyes for a big surprise!'

William certainly would be surprised at what a rotten treat he'd be getting.

Weepy William put down his swag bag, closed his eyes tight, then plunged his hand into Henry's lucky dip. He rummaged and he rummaged and he rummaged, hoping to find something better than satsumas.

Horrid Henry eyed Weepy William's bulging swag bag.

Go on, Henry, urged the bag. He'll never notice.

Horrid Henry did not wait to be asked twice.

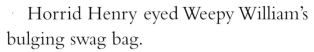

Horrid Henry grabbed a big handful of William's sweets and popped them inside his empty bag.

Weepy William opened his eyes.

'Did you take some of my sweets?'

'No,' said Henry.

William peeked inside his bag and burst into tears.

'Waaaaaaaa!' wailed William. 'Henry took –'

Henry pushed him out and slammed the door.

Dad came running.

'What's wrong?'

'Nothing,' said Henry. 'Just William crying 'cause he's scared of pumpkins.'

Phew, thought Henry. That was close. Perhaps he had been a little too greedy.

Ding dong.

 It was Lazy Linda wearing a pillowcase over her head.

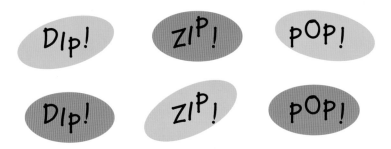 Gorgeous Gurinder was with her, dressed as a scarecrow.

'Trick-or-treat!'

'Trick-or-treat!'

'Close your eyes for a big surprise!' said Henry, holding out the lucky dip bag.

'Ooh, a lucky dip!' squealed Linda.

Lazy Linda and Gorgeous Gurinder put down their bags, closed their eyes, and reached into the lucky dip.

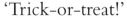 Dip! ZIP! POP!

Dip! ZIP! POP!

Lazy Linda opened her eyes.

'You give the worst treats ever, Henry,' said Linda, gazing at her walnut in disgust.

'We won't be coming back *here*,' sniffed Gorgeous Gurinder.

Tee hee, thought Horrid Henry.

Ding dong.

It was Beefy Bert. He was wearing a robot costume.

'Hi, Bert, got any good sweets?' asked Henry.

'I dunno,' said Beefy Bert.

Horrid Henry soon found out that he did. Lots and lots and lots of them. So did Moody Margaret, Sour Susan, Jolly Josh and Tidy Ted. Soon Henry's bag was stuffed with treats.

Ding dong.

Horrid Henry opened the door.

'Boo,' said Atomic Bunny.

Henry's sweet bag! Help! Mum would see it!

'Eeeeek!' screeched Horrid Henry. 'Help! Save me!'

Quickly, he ran upstairs clutching his bag and hid it safely under his bed. Phew, that was close.

'Don't be scared, Henry, it's only me,' called Perfect Peter.

Horrid Henry came back downstairs.

'No!' said Henry. 'I'd never have known.'

'Really?' said Peter.

'Really,' said Henry.

'Everyone just gave sweets this year,' said Perfect Peter. 'Yuck.'

Horrid Henry held out the lucky dip.

'Ooh, a satsuma,' said Peter. 'Aren't I lucky!'

'I hope you've learned your lesson, Henry,' said Mum sternly.

'I certainly have,' said Horrid Henry, eyeing Perfect Peter's bulging bag. 'Good things come to those who wait.'

SHOPPING LIST

Muesli
Carrots
Wholemeal Bread
Spinach
Eggs
Chicken
Raisins

Pickeled Union Crisps
Chocolit eyeballs
Chocolit cake
Crunchy crakkers
Sweet Tweets
Jumbo Pack of Big Boppers

HORRID HENRY
AND THE
MUMMY'S CURSE

iptoe. Tiptoe. Tiptoe.

Horrid Henry crept down the hall. The coast
was clear. Mum and Dad were in the garden, and Peter
was playing at Tidy Ted's.

Tee hee, thought Henry, then darted into Perfect
Peter's room and shut the door.

There it was. Sitting unopened on Peter's shelf. The
grossest, yuckiest, most stomach-curdling kit Henry had
ever seen. A brand-new, deluxe Curse of the Mummy
kit, complete with a plastic body to mummify,
mummy-wrapping gauze, curse book, amulets and,
best of all, removable mummy organs to put in a
canopic jar. Peter had won it at the 'Meet a Real
Mummy' exhibition at the museum, but he'd never
even played with it once.

Of course, Henry wasn't allowed into Peter's bedroom without permission. He was also not allowed to play with Peter's toys. This was so unfair, Henry could hardly believe it. True, he wouldn't let Peter touch his Boom-Boom Basher, his Goo-Shooter, or his Dungeon Drink kit. In fact, since Henry refused to share *any* of his toys with Peter, Mum had forbidden Henry to play with any of Peter's toys – or else.

Henry didn't care – Perfect Peter had boring baby toys – until, that is, he brought home the mummy kit. Henry had ached to play with it. And now was his chance.

Horrid Henry tore off the wrapping, and opened the box.

WOW! So gross! Henry felt a delicious shiver. He loved mummies. What could be more thrilling than looking at an ancient, wrapped-up DEAD body? Even a pretend one was wonderful. And now he had hours of fun ahead of him.

Pitter-patter! Pitter-patter! Pitter-patter!

Oh help, someone was coming up the stairs! Horrid
Henry shoved the mummy kit behind him as Peter's
bedroom door swung open and Perfect Peter strolled in.

'Out of my way, worm!' shouted Henry.

Perfect Peter slunk off. Then he stopped.

'Wait a minute,' he said. 'You're in *my* room! You
can't order me out of my own room!'

'Oh yeah?' blustered Henry.

'Yeah!' said Peter.

'You're supposed to be at Ted's,' said Henry, trying
to distract him.

'He got sick,' said Peter. He stepped closer. 'And
you're playing with my kit! You're not allowed to play
with any of my things! Mum said so! I'm going to tell
her right now!'

Uh oh. If Peter told on him Henry would be in big
trouble. Very big trouble. Henry had to save himself,
fast. He had two choices. He could leap on Peter and
throttle him. Or he could use weasel words.

'I wasn't playing with it,' said Henry smoothly. 'I was trying to protect you.'

'No you weren't,' said Peter. 'I'm telling.'

'I was, too,' said Henry. 'I was trying to protect you from the Mummy's Curse.'

Perfect Peter headed for the door. Then he stopped.

'What curse?' said Peter.

'The curse which turns people into mummies!' said Henry desperately.

'There's no such thing,' said Peter.

'Wanna bet?' said Henry. 'Everyone knows about the mummy's curse! They take on the shape of someone familiar but really, they're mummies! They could be your cat —'

'Fluffy?' said Peter. 'Fluffy, a mummy?'

Henry looked at fat Fluffy snoring peacefully on a cushion.

'Even Fluffy,' said Henry. 'Or Dad. Or me. Or you.'

'I'm not a mummy,' said Peter.

'Or even –' Henry paused melodramatically and then whispered, 'Mum.'

'Mum, a mummy?' gasped Peter.

'Yup,' said Henry. 'But don't worry. You help me draw some Eyes of Horus. They'll protect us against . . . her.'

'She's not a mummy,' said Peter.

'That's what she wants us to think,' whispered Henry. 'It's all here in the Mummy curse book.' He waved the book in front of Peter. 'Don't you think the mummy on the cover resembles you-know-who?'

'No,' said Peter.

'Watch,' said Horrid Henry. He grabbed a pencil.

'Don't draw on a book!' squeaked Peter.

Henry ignored him and drew glasses on the mummy.

'How about now?' he asked.

Peter stared. Was it his imagination or did the mummy look a little familiar?

'I don't believe you,' said Peter. 'I'm going straight down to ask Mum.'

'But that's the worst thing you could do!' shouted Henry.

'I don't care,' said Peter. Down he went.

Henry was sunk. Mum would probably cancel his birthday party when Peter blabbed. And he'd never even had a chance to play with the mummy kit! It was so unfair.

Mum was reading on the sofa.

'Mum,' said Peter, 'Henry says you're a mummy.'

Mum looked puzzled.

'Of course I'm a mummy,' she said.

'What?' said Peter.

'I'm your mummy,' said Mum, with a smile.

Peter took a step back.

'I don't want you to be a mummy,' said Peter.

'But I am one,' said Mum. 'Now come and give me a hug.'

'No!' said Peter.

'Let me wrap my arms around you,' said Mum.

'NO WRAPPING!' squealed Peter. 'I want my mummy!'

'But I'm your mummy,' said Mum.

'I know!' squeaked Peter. 'Keep away, you . . . mummy!'

Perfect Peter staggered up the stairs to Henry.

'It's true,' he gasped. 'She said she was a mummy.'

'She did?' said Henry.

'Yes,' said Peter. 'What are we going to do?'

'Don't worry, Peter,' said Henry. 'We can free her from the curse.'

'How?' breathed Peter.

Horrid Henry pretended to consult the curse book.

'First we must sacrifice to the Egyptian gods Osiris and Hroth,' said Henry.

'Sacrifice?' said Peter.

'They like cat guts, and stuff like that,' said Henry.

'No!' squealed Peter. 'Not . . . Fluffy!'

'However,' said Henry, leafing through the curse book, 'marbles are also acceptable as an offering.'

Perfect Peter ran to his toybox and scooped up a handful of marbles.

'Now fetch me some loo roll,' added Henry.

'Loo roll?' said Peter.

'Do not question the priest of Anubis!' shrieked Henry.

Perfect Peter fetched the loo roll.

'We must wrap Fluffy in the sacred bandages,' said Henry. 'He will be our messenger between this world and the next.'

'Meoww,' said Fluffy, as he was wrapped from head to tail in loo paper.

'Now you,' said Henry.

'Me?' squeaked Peter.

'Yes,' said Henry. 'Do you want to free Mum from the mummy's curse?'

Peter nodded.

'Then you must stand still and be quiet for thirty minutes,' said Henry. That should give him plenty of time to have a go with the mummy kit.

He started wrapping Peter. Round and round and round and round went the loo roll until Peter was tightly trussed from head to toe.

Henry stepped back to admire his work. Goodness, he was a brilliant mummy-maker! Maybe that's what he should be when he grew up. Henry, the Mummy-Maker. Henry, World's Finest Mummy-Maker. Henry, Mummy-Maker to the Stars. Yes, it certainly had a ring to it.

'You're a fine-looking mummy, Peter,' said Henry. 'I'm sure you'll be made very welcome in the next world.'

'Huuunh?' said Peter.

'Silence!' ordered Henry. 'Don't move. Now I must utter the sacred spell. By the powers of Horus, Morus, Borus and Stegosaurus,' intoned Henry, making up all the Egyptian sounding names he could.

'Stegosaurus?' mumbled Peter.

'Whatever!' snapped Henry. 'I call on the scarab! I call on Isis! Free Fluffy from the mummy's curse. Free Peter from the mummy's curse. Free Mum from the mummy's curse. Free –'

'What on earth is going on in here?' shrieked Mum, bursting through the door. 'You horrid boy! What have you done to Peter? And what have you done to poor Fluffy?'

'Meoww,' yowled Fluffy.

'Mummy!' squealed Perfect Peter.

MEOWW

Eowww, gross! thought Horrid Henry, opening up the plastic mummy body and placing the organs in the canopic jar.

The bad news was that Henry had been banned from watching TV for a week. The good news was that Perfect Peter had said he never wanted to see that horrible mummy kit again.

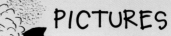

HORRID HENRY'S
BIRTHDAY PARTY

February was Horrid Henry's favourite month.

His birthday was in February.

'It's my birthday soon!' said Henry every day after Christmas. 'And my birthday party! Hurray!'

February was Horrid Henry's parents' least favourite month.

'It's Henry's birthday soon,' said Dad, groaning.

'And his birthday party,' said Mum, groaning even louder.

Every year they thought Henry's birthday parties could not get worse. But they always did.

Every year Henry's parents said they would never ever let Henry have a birthday party again. But every year they gave Henry one absolutely last final chance.

Henry had big plans for this year's party.

'I want to go to Lazer Zap,' said Henry. He'd been to Lazer Zap for Tough Toby's party. They'd had a great time dressing up as spacemen and blasting each other in dark tunnels all afternoon.

'NO!' said Mum. 'Too violent.'

'I agree,' said Dad.

'And too expensive,' said Mum.

'I agree,' said Dad.

There was a moment's silence.

'However,' said Dad, 'it does mean the party wouldn't be here.'

Mum looked at Dad. Dad looked at Mum.

'How do I book?' said Mum.

'Hurray!' shrieked Henry. 'Zap! Zap! Zap!'

Horrid Henry sat in his fort holding a pad of paper. On the front cover in big capital letters Henry wrote:

At the top of the first page Henry wrote:

Guests

A long list followed. Then Henry stared at the names and chewed his pencil.

Actually, I don't want Margaret, thought Henry. Too moody.

He crossed out Moody Margaret's name.

And I definitely don't want Susan. Too crabby.

In fact, I don't want any girls at all, thought Henry. He crossed out Clever Clare and Lazy Linda.

Then there was Anxious Andrew.

Nope, thought Henry, crossing him off. He's no fun.

Toby was possible, but Henry didn't really like him. Out went Tough Toby.

William?

No way, thought Henry. He'll be crying the second he gets zapped.

Out went Weepy William.

Ralph?

Henry considered. Ralph would be good because he was sure to get into trouble. On the other hand, he hadn't invited Henry to *his* party.

Rude Ralph was struck off.

So were Babbling Bob, Jolly Josh, Greedy Graham and Dizzy Dave. And absolutely no way was Peter coming anywhere near him on his birthday.

Ahh, that was better. No horrid kids would be coming to *his* party.

Henry's Party Plans
TOP Secret

Guests

~~Margaret~~
~~Susan~~
~~Clare~~
~~Linda~~
~~Andrew~~
~~Toby~~
~~William~~
~~Ralph~~
~~Bob~~
~~Josh~~
~~Graham~~
~~Dave~~
~~Peter~~

There was only one problem. Every single name was crossed off.

No guests meant no presents.

Henry looked at his list. Margaret was a moody old grouch and he hated her, but she did sometimes give good gifts. He still had the jumbo box of day-glo slime she'd given him last year.

And Toby *had* invited Henry to *his* party.

And Dave was always spinning round like a top, falling and knocking things over which was fun. Graham would eat too much and burp. And Ralph was sure to say rude words and make all the grown-ups angry.

Oh, let them all come, thought Henry. Except Peter, of course. The more guests I have, the more presents I get!

Henry turned to the next page and wrote:

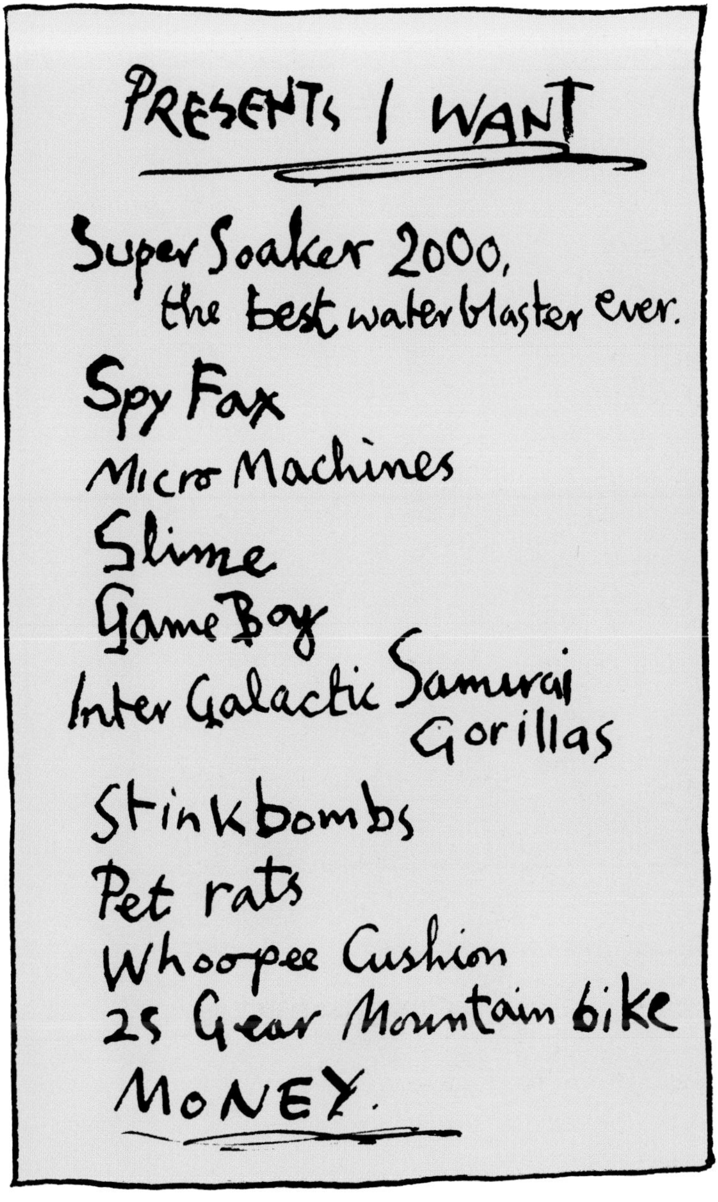

PRESENTS I WANT

Super Soaker 2000, the best water blaster ever.

Spy Fax

Micro Machines

Slime

Game Boy

Inter Galactic Samurai Gorillas

Stinkbombs

Pet rats

Whoopee Cushion

25 Gear Mountain bike

MONEY.

He'd leave the list lying around where Mum and Dad were sure to find it.

'I've done the menu for the party,' said Mum. 'What do you think?'

Mum's Menu

carrot sticks
cucumber sandwiches
grapes
raisins
apple juice
carrot cake

'Blecccccch,' said Henry. 'I don't want that horrible food at my party. I want food that I like.'

Henry's Menu

Pickled Onion Monster
Munch

Smoky Spider Shreddies

Super Spicy Hedgehog Crisps

Crunchy Crackles

Twizzle Fizzle Sticks

Purple Planet-buster Drink

Chocolate bars

Chocolate eggs

Chocolate Monster Cake

'You can't just have junk food,' said Mum.

'It's not junk food,' said Henry. 'Crisps are made from potatoes, and Monster Munch has onions – that's two vegetables.'

'Henry . . .' said Mum. She looked fierce.

Henry looked at his menu. Then he added, in small letters at the bottom:

peanut butter sandwiches

'But only in the middle of the table,' said Henry. 'So no one has to eat them who doesn't want them.'

'All right,' said Mum. Years of fighting with Henry about his parties had worn her down.

'And Peter's not coming,' said Henry.

'What?!' said Perfect Peter, looking up from polishing his shoes.

'Peter is your brother. Of course he's invited.'

Henry scowled.

'But he'll ruin everything.'

'No Peter, no party,' said Mum.

Henry pretended he was a fire-breathing dragon.

'Owww!' shrieked Peter.

'Don't be horrid, Henry!' yelled Mum.

'All right,' said Henry. 'He can come. But you'd better keep out of my way,' he hissed at Peter.

'Mum!' wailed Peter. 'Henry's being mean to me.

'Stop it, Henry,' said Mum.

Henry decided to change the subject fast.

'What about party bags?' said Henry. 'I want everyone to have Slime, and loads and loads and loads of sweets! Dirt Balls, Nose Pickers and Foam Teeth are the best.'

'We'll see,' said Mum. She looked at the calendar. Only two more days. Soon it would be over.

Henry's birthday arrived at last.

'Happy birthday, Henry!' said Mum.

'Happy birthday, Henry!' said Dad.

'Happy birthday, Henry!' said Peter.

'Where are my presents?' said Henry.

Dad pointed. Horrid Henry attacked the pile.

Mum and Dad had given him a *First Encyclopedia*,

Scrabble, a fountain pen, a hand-knitted cardigan, a globe, and three sets of vests and pants.

'Oh,' said Henry. He pushed the dreadful presents aside.

'Anything else?' he asked hopefully. Maybe they were keeping the super soaker for last.

'I've got a present for you,' said Peter. 'I chose it myself.'

Henry tore off the wrapping paper. It was a tapestry kit.

'Yuck!' said Henry.

'I'll have it if you don't want it,' said Peter.

'No!' said Henry, snatching up the kit.

'Wasn't it a great idea to have Henry's party at Lazer Zap?' said Dad.

'Yes,' said Mum. 'No mess, no fuss.'

They smiled at each other.

Ring ring.

Dad answered the phone. It was the Lazer Zap lady.

'Hello! I was just ringing to check the birthday boy's name,' she said. 'We like to announce it over our loudspeaker during the party.'

Dad gave Henry's name.

A terrible scream came from the other end of the phone. Dad held the receiver away from his ear.

The shrieking and screaming continued.

'Hmmmn,' said Dad. 'I see. Thank you.'

Dad hung up. He looked pale.

'Henry!'

'Yeah?'

'Is it true that you wrecked the place when you went to Lazer Zap with Toby?' said Dad.

'No!' said Henry. He tried to look harmless.

'And trampled on several children?'

'No!' said Henry.

'Yes you did,' said Perfect Peter. 'And what about all the lasers you broke?'

'What lasers?' said Henry.

'And the slime you put in the space suits?' said Peter.

'That wasn't me, telltale,' shrieked Henry. 'What about my party?'

'I'm afraid Lazer Zap have banned you,' said Dad.

'But what about Henry's party?' said Mum. She looked pale.

'But what about my party?!' wailed Henry. 'I want to go to Lazer Zap!'

'Never mind,' said Dad brightly. 'I know lots of good games.'

Ding dong.

It was the first guest, Sour Susan. She held a large present.

Henry snatched the package.

It was a pad of paper and some felt tip pens.

'How lovely,' said Mum. 'What do you say, Henry?'

'I've already got that,' said Henry.

'Henry!' said Mum. 'Don't be horrid!'

I don't care, thought Henry. This was the worst day of his life.

Ding dong.

It was the second guest, Anxious Andrew. He held a tiny present.

Henry snatched the package.

'It's awfully small,' said Henry, tearing off the wrapping. 'And it smells.'

It was a box of animal soaps.

'How super,' said Dad. 'What do you say, Henry?'

'Ugghhh!' said Henry.

'Henry!' said Dad. 'Don't be horrid.'

Henry stuck out his lower lip.

'It's my party and I'll do what I want,' muttered Henry.

'Watch your step, young man,' said Dad.

Henry stuck out his tongue behind Dad's back.

More guests arrived.

Lazy Linda gave him a 'Read and Listen Cassette of Favourite Fairy Tales: Cinderella, Snow White and Sleeping Beauty'.

'Fabulous,' said Mum.

'Yuck!' said Henry.

Clever Clare handed him a square package.

Henry held it by the corners.

'It's a book,' he groaned.

'My favourite present!' said Peter.

'Wonderful,' said Mum. 'What is it?'

Henry unwrapped it slowly.

'Cook Your Own Healthy Nutritious Food.'

'Great!' said Perfect Peter. 'Can I borrow it?'

'NO!' screamed Henry. Then he threw the book on the floor and stomped on it.

'Henry!' hissed Mum. 'I'm warning you. When someone gives you a present you say thank you.'

Rude Ralph was the last to arrive.

He handed Henry a long rectangular package wrapped in newspaper.

It was a Super Soaker 2000 water blaster.

'Oh,' said Mum.

'Put it away,' said Dad.

'Thank you, Ralph,' beamed Henry. 'Just what I wanted.'

'Let's start with Pass the Parcel,' said Dad.

'I hate Pass the Parcel,' said Horrid Henry. What a horrible party this was.

'I love Pass the Parcel,' said Perfect Peter.

'I don't want to play,' said Sour Susan.

'When do we eat?' said Greedy Graham.

Dad started the music.

'Pass the parcel, William,' said Dad.

'No!' shrieked William. 'It's mine!'

'But the music is still playing,' said Dad.

William burst into tears.

Horrid Henry tried to snatch the parcel.

Dad stopped the music.

William stopped crying instantly and tore off the wrapping.

'A granola bar,' he said.

'That's a terrible prize,' said Rude Ralph.

'Is it my turn yet?' said Anxious Andrew.

'When do we eat?' said Greedy Graham.

'I hate Pass the Parcel,' screamed Henry. 'I want to play something else.'

'Musical Statues!' announced Mum brightly.

'You're out, Henry,' said Dad. 'You moved.'

'I didn't,' said Henry.

'Yes you did,' said Toby.

'No I didn't,' said Henry. 'I'm not leaving.'

'That's not fair,' shrieked Sour Susan.

'I'm not playing,' whined Dizzy Dave.

'I'm tired,' sulked Lazy Linda.

'I hate Musical Statues,' moaned Moody Margaret.

'Where's my prize?' demanded Rude Ralph.

'A bookmark?' said Ralph. 'That's it?'

'Tea time!' said Dad.

The children pushed and shoved their way to the table, grabbing and snatching at the food.

'I hate fizzy drinks,' said Tough Toby.

'I feel sick,' said Greedy Graham.

'Where are the carrot sticks?' said Perfect Peter.

Horrid Henry sat at the head of the table.

He didn't feel like throwing food at Clare.

He didn't feel like rampaging with Toby and Ralph.

He didn't even feel like kicking Peter.

He wanted to be at Lazer Zap.

Then Henry had a wonderful, spectacular idea. He got up and sneaked out of the room.

'Party bags,' said Dad.

'What's in them?' said Tough Toby.

'Seedlings,' said Mum.

'Where are the sweets?' said Greedy Graham.

'This is the worst party bag I've ever had,' said Rude Ralph.

There was a noise outside.

Then Henry burst into the kitchen, supersoaker in hand.

'ZAP! ZAP! ZAP!' shrieked Henry, drenching everyone with water. 'Ha! Ha! Gotcha!'

Splat went the cake.

Splash went the drinks.

'EEEEEEEEEEEEKKK!' shrieked the sopping wet children.

'HENRY!!!!!' yelled Mum and Dad.

'YOU HORRID BOY!' yelled Mum. Water dripped from her hair. 'GO TO YOUR ROOM!'

'THIS IS YOUR LAST PARTY EVER!' yelled Dad. Water dripped from his clothes.

But Henry didn't care. They said that every year.

STAR CHART

Henry.	
Monday	
Tuesday	
Wednesday	
Thursday	★ ← putting fork
Friday	for in dishwasher
Saturday	
Sunday	

Peter.	
Monday	★ ★ ★ ★
Tuesday	★ ★ ★ ★ ★
Wednesday	★ ★ ★ ★
Thursday	★ ★★ ★
Friday	★ ★ ★ ★ ★
Saturday	★ ★★ ★
Sunday	★ ★ ★ ★ ★ ★

Dear Mum and Dad
NO thank you for the vests,
Socks and books.
BLEUCCCCCK.
Why do I always get
Such yucky presents.
£10 is FAR too little.
Henry

HORRID HENRY'S THANK YOU LETTER

Ahh! This was the life! A sofa, a telly, a bag of crisps. Horrid Henry sighed happily.

'Henry!' shouted Mum from the kitchen. 'Are you watching TV?'

Henry blocked his ears. Nothing was going to interrupt his new favourite TV programme, *Terminator Gladiator*.

'Answer me, Henry!' shouted Mum. 'Have you written your Christmas thank you letters?'

'NO!' bellowed Henry.

'Why not?' screamed Mum.

'Because I haven't,' said Henry. 'I'm busy.' Couldn't she leave him alone for two seconds?

Mum marched into the room and switched off the TV.

'Hey!' said Henry. 'I'm watching *Terminator Gladiator.*'

'Too bad,' said Mum. 'I told you, no TV until you've written your thank you letters.'

'It's not fair!' wailed Henry.

'I've written all *my* thank you letters,' said Perfect Peter.

'Well done, Peter,' said Mum. 'Thank goodness *one* of my children has good manners.'

Peter smiled modestly. 'I always write mine the moment I unwrap a present. I'm a good boy, aren't I?'

'The best,' said Mum.

'Oh, shut up, Peter,' snarled Henry.

'Mum! Henry told me to shut up!' said Peter.

'Stop being horrid, Henry. You will write to Aunt Ruby, Great-Aunt Greta and Grandma now.'

'Now?' moaned Henry. 'Can't I do it later?'

'When's later?' said Dad.

'Later!' said Henry. Why wouldn't they stop nagging him about those stupid letters?

Horrid Henry hated writing thank you letters. Why should he waste his precious time saying thank you for presents? Time he could be spending reading comics, or watching TV. But no. He would barely unwrap a present before Mum started nagging. She even expected him to write to Great-Aunt Greta and thank her for the Baby Poopie Pants doll. Great-Aunt Greta for one did not deserve a thank you letter.

This year Aunt Ruby had sent him a hideous lime green cardigan. Why should he thank her for that?

True, Grandma had given him £15, which was great. But then Mum had to spoil it by making him write her a letter too. Henry hated writing letters for nice presents every bit as much as he hated writing them for horrible ones.

'You have to write thank you letters,' said Dad.

'But why?' said Henry.

'Because it's polite,' said Dad.

'Because people have spent time and money on you,' said Mum.

So what? thought Horrid Henry. Grown-ups had loads of time to do whatever they wanted. No one told them, stop watching TV and write a thank you letter. Oh no. They could do it whenever they felt like it. Or not even do it at all.

And adults had tons of money compared to him. Why shouldn't they spend it buying him presents?

'All you have to do is write one page,' said Dad. 'What's the big deal?'

Henry stared at him. Did Dad have no idea how long it would take him to write one whole page? Hours and hours and hours.

'You're the meanest, most horrible parents in the world and I hate you!' shrieked Horrid Henry.

'Go to your room, Henry!' shouted Dad.

'And don't come down until you've written those letters,' shouted Mum. 'I am sick and tired of arguing about this.'

Horrid Henry stomped upstairs.

Well, no way was he writing any thank you letters. He'd rather starve. He'd rather die. He'd stay in his room for a month. A year. One day Mum and Dad would come up to check on him and all they'd find would be a few bones. Then they'd be sorry.

Actually, knowing them, they'd probably just moan about the mess. And then Peter would be all happy because he'd get Henry's room and Henry's room was bigger.

Well, no way would he give them the satisfaction. All right, thought Horrid Henry. Dad said to write one page. Henry would write one page. In his biggest, most gigantic handwriting, Henry wrote:

That certainly filled a whole page, thought Horrid Henry.

Mum came into the room.

'Have you written your letters yet?'

'Yes,' lied Henry.

Mum glanced over his shoulder.

'Henry!' said Mum. 'That is not a proper thank you letter.'

'Yes it is,' snarled Henry. 'Dad said to write one page so I wrote one page.'

'Write five sentences,' said Mum.

Five sentences? Five whole sentences? It was completely impossible for anyone to write so much. His hand would fall off.

'That's way too much,' wailed Henry.

'No TV until you write your letters,' said Mum, leaving the room.

Horrid Henry stuck out his tongue. He had the meanest, most horrible parents in the world. When he was King any parent who even whispered the words 'thank you letter' would get fed to the crocodiles.

They wanted five sentences? He'd give them five sentences. Henry picked up his pencil and scrawled:

Dear Aunt Ruby,
No thank you for the horrible present. It is the worst present I have ever had. Anyway, didn't some old Roman say it was better to give than to receive? So in fact, you should be writing me a thank you letter.
    Henry
P.S. Next time just send money.

There! Five whole sentences. Perfect, thought Horrid Henry. Mum said he had to write a five-sentence thank you letter. She never said it had to be a *nice* thank you letter. Suddenly Henry felt quite cheerful. He folded the letter and popped it in the stamped envelope Mum had given him.

One down. Two to go.

In fact, Aunt Ruby's no thank you letter would do just fine for Great-Aunt Greta. He'd just substitute Great-Aunt Greta's name for Aunt Ruby's and copy the rest.

Bingo. Another letter was done.

Now, Grandma. She *had* sent money so he'd have to write something nice.

'Thank you for the money, blah blah blah, best present I've ever received, blah blah blah, next year send more money, £15 isn't very much, Ralph got £20 from *his* grandma, blah blah blah.'

What a waste, thought Horrid Henry as he signed it and put it in the envelope, to spend so much time on a letter, only to have to write the same old thing all over again next year.

And then suddenly Horrid Henry had a wonderful, spectacular idea. Why had he never thought of this before? He would be rich, rich, rich. 'There goes money-bags Henry,' kids would whisper enviously, as he swaggered down the street, followed by Peter lugging a hundred videos for Henry to watch in his

mansion on one of his twenty-eight giant TVs. Mum and Dad and Peter would be living in their hovel somewhere, and if they were very, very nice to him Henry *might* let them watch one of his smaller TVs for fifteen minutes or so once a month.

Henry was going to start a business. A business guaranteed to make him rich.

'Step right up, step right up,' said Horrid Henry. He was wearing a sign saying: 'HENRY'S THANK YOU LETTERS: Personal letters written just for you.' A small crowd of children gathered round him.

'I'll write all your thank you letters for you,' said Henry. 'All you have to do is to give me a stamped, addressed envelope and tell me what present you got.

I'll do the rest.'

'How much for a thank you letter?' asked Kung-Fu Kate.

'A pound,' said Henry.

'No way,' said Greedy Graham.

'99p,' said Henry.

'Forget it,' said Lazy Linda.

'OK, 50p,' said Henry. 'And two for 75p.'

'Done,' said Linda.

Henry opened his notebook. 'And what were the presents?' he asked. Linda made a face. 'Handkerchiefs,' she spat. 'And a bookmark.'

'I can do a "no thank you" letter,' said Henry. 'I'm very good at those.' Linda considered.

'Tempting,' she said, 'but then mean Uncle John won't send something better next time.'

Business was brisk. Dave bought three. Ralph bought four 'no thank you's. Even Moody Margaret bought one. Whoopee, thought Horrid Henry. His pockets were jingle-jangling with cash. Now all he had to do was to write seventeen letters. Henry tried not to think about that.

The moment he got home from school Henry went straight to his room. Right, to work, thought Henry. His heart sank as he looked at the blank pages. All those letters! He would be here for weeks. Why had he ever set up a letter-writing business?

But then Horrid Henry thought. True, he'd promised a personal letter but how would Linda's aunt ever find out that Margaret's granny had received the same one? She wouldn't! If he used the computer, it would be a cinch. And it would be a letter sent personally, thought Henry, because I am a person and I will personally print it out and send it. All he'd have to do was to write the names at the top and to sign them. Easy-peasy lemon squeezy.

Then again, all that signing. And writing all those names at the top. And separating the thank you letters from the no thank you ones.

Maybe there was a better way.

Horrid Henry sat down at the computer and typed:

Dear Sir or Madam,

That should cover everyone, thought Henry, and I won't have to write anyone's name.

Thank you/No thank you for the
a) wonderful
b) horrible
c) disgusting
present. I really loved it/hated it. In fact, it is the best present/worst present I have ever received. I played with it/broke it/ate it/spent it/threw it in the bin straight away. Next time just send lots of money.
Best wishes/worst wishes

Now, how to sign it? Aha, thought Henry.

Your friend or relative.

Perfect, thought Horrid Henry. Sir or Madam knows whether they deserve a thank you or a no thank you letter. Let them do some work for a change and tick the correct answers.

Out spewed seventeen letters. It only took a moment to stuff them in the envelopes. He'd pop the letters in the postbox on the way to school.

Had an easier way to become a
millionaire ever been invented? thought Horrid
Henry, as he turned on the telly.

Ding dong.

It was two weeks after Henry set up 'Henry's
Thank You Letters'.

Horrid Henry opened the door.

A group of Henry's customers stood there, waving
pieces of paper and shouting.

'My granny sent the letter back and now I can't
watch TV for a week,' wailed Moody Margaret.

'I'm grounded!' screamed Aerobic Al.

'I have to go swimming!' screamed Lazy Linda.

'No sweets!' yelped Greedy Graham.

'No pocket money!' screamed Rude Ralph.

'And it's all your fault!' they shouted.

Horrid Henry glared at his angry customers. He was outraged. After all his hard work, *this* was the thanks he got?

'Too bad!' said Horrid Henry as he slammed the door. Honestly, there was no pleasing some people.

'Henry,' said Mum. 'I just had the strangest phone call from Aunt Ruby . . .'

Holiday Snaps

JOKES NOT TO TELL AUNT RUBY

MUM: Henry! I've just had the strangest call from Aunt Ruby . . .
HENRY: Hide!

What do you call an aunt on the toilet?
Lou Lou.

What do you call an aunt who falls off the toilet?
Lou Roll.

Why do you put your aunt in the fridge?
To make Auntie-freeze.

Has your aunt caught up with you yet?
No, but when she does I'm going to need a lot of Auntie-septic.

How do you make anti-freeze?
Hide her nightie.

166

How can you tell if Aunt Ruby's been to visit?
She's still in the house.

MUM: Henry, we're having Aunt Ruby for lunch this
Sunday.
HENRY: **Can't we have roast beef instead?**

MUM: Henry! Why did you put a slug in
Aunt Ruby's bed?
HENRY: **I couldn't find
a snake.**

AUNT RUBY: Goodness! It's raining cats and dogs.
HENRY: **I know. I nearly stepped in a
poodle.**

AUNT RUBY: Well, Henry,
I'm leaving tomorrow.
Are you sorry?

HENRY: **Oh yes,
Aunt Ruby,
I thought you were
leaving
today.**

*Not
Suitable
for
Aunts*

Dear Father Christmas
I don't understand why
you didn't bring me the
Robomatic Supersonic Space
Howler I askd for.
I wrote it in HUG-E letters.
Can't you read?
It had better not happen
again.
    You have been Warned.
                    Henry

HORRID HENRY'S HOLIDAY

Horrid Henry hated holidays.

Henry's idea of a super holiday was sitting on the sofa eating crisps and watching TV.

Unfortunately, his parents usually had other plans.

Once they took him to see some castles. But there were no castles. There were only piles of stones and broken walls.

'Never again,' said Henry.

The next year he had to go to a lot of museums.

'Never again,' said Mum and Dad.

Last year they went to the seaside.

'The sun is too hot,' Henry whined.

'The water is too cold,' Henry whinged.

'The food is yucky,' Henry grumbled.

'The bed is lumpy,' Henry moaned.

This year they decided to try something different.

'We're going camping in France,' said Henry's parents.

'Hooray!' said Henry.

'You're happy, Henry?' said Mum. Henry had never been happy about any holiday plans before.

'Oh yes,' said Henry. Finally, finally, they were doing something good.

Henry knew all about camping from Moody
Margaret. Margaret had been camping with her family.
They had stayed in a big tent with comfy beds, a fridge,
a cooker, a loo, a shower, a heated swimming pool, a
disco and a great big giant TV with fifty-seven channels.

'Oh boy!' said Horrid Henry.

'Bonjour!' said Perfect Peter.

The great day arrived at last. Horrid Henry, Perfect
Peter, Mum and Dad boarded the ferry for France.

Henry and Peter had never been on a boat before.
Henry jumped on and off the seats.

Peter did a lovely drawing.

The
boat went
up and
down and
up and
down.

Henry ran back and forth
between the aisles.

Peter pasted stickers in his
notebook.

The boat went up and down
and up and down.

Henry sat on a revolving
chair and spun round.

Peter played with his
puppets.

The boat went up and down and up and down.

Then Henry and Peter ate a big greasy lunch of sausages and chips in the café.

The boat went up and down, and up and down, and up and down.

Henry began to feel queasy.

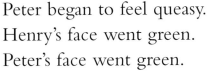

Peter began to feel queasy. Henry's face went green. Peter's face went green.

'I think I'm going to be sick,' said Henry, and threw up all over Mum.

'I think I'm going to be –' said Peter, and threw up all over Dad.

'Oh no,' said Mum.

'Never mind,' said Dad. 'I just know this will be our best holiday ever.'

Finally, the boat arrived in France.

After driving and driving and driving they reached the campsite.

It was even better than Henry's dreams. The tents were as big as houses. Henry heard the happy sound of TVs blaring, music playing, and children splashing and shrieking. The sun shone. The sky was blue.

'Wow, this looks great,' said Henry.

But the car drove on.

'Stop!' said Henry. 'You've gone too far.'

'We're not staying in that awful place,' said Dad.

They drove on.

'Here's our campsite,' said Dad. 'A *real* campsite!'

Henry stared at the bare rocky ground under the cloudy grey sky.

There were three small tents flapping in the wind. There was a single tap. There were a few trees. There was nothing else.

'It's wonderful!' said Mum.

'It's wonderful!' said Peter.

'But where's the TV?' said Henry.

'No TV here, thank goodness,' said Mum. 'We've got books.'

'But where are the beds?' said Henry.

'No beds here, thank goodness,' said Dad. 'We've got sleeping bags.'

'But where's the pool?' said Henry.

'No pool,' said Dad. '*We'll* swim in the river.'

'Where's the toilet?' said Peter.

Dad pointed at a distant cubicle. Three people stood waiting.

'All the way over there?' said Peter. 'I'm not complaining,' he added quickly.

Mum and Dad unpacked the car. Henry stood and scowled.

'Who wants to help put up the tent?' asked Mum.

'I do!' said Dad.

'I do!' said Peter.

Henry was horrified. 'We have to put up our own tent?'

'Of course,' said Mum.

'I don't like it here,' said Henry. 'I want to go camping in the other place.'

'That's not camping,' said Dad. 'Those tents have beds in them. And loos. And showers. And fridges. And cookers, and TVs. Horrible.' Dad shuddered.

'Horrible,' said Peter.

'And we have such a lovely snug tent here,' said Mum. 'Nothing modern – just wooden pegs and poles.'

'Well, I want to stay there,' said Henry.

'We're staying here,' said Dad.

'NO!' screamed Henry.

'YES!' screamed Dad.

I am sorry to say that Henry then had the longest, loudest, noisiest, shrillest, most horrible tantrum you can imagine.

Did you think that a horrid boy like Henry would like nothing better than sleeping on hard rocky ground in a soggy sleeping bag without a pillow?

You thought wrong.

Henry liked comfy beds.

Henry liked crisp sheets.

Henry liked hot baths.

Henry liked microwave dinners, TV, and noise.

He did not like cold showers, fresh air, and quiet.

Far off in the distance the sweet sound of loud music drifted towards them.

'Aren't you glad we're not staying in that awful noisy place?' said Dad.

'Oh yes,' said Mum.

'Oh yes,' said Perfect Peter.

Henry pretended he was a bulldozer come to knock down tents and squash campers.

'Henry, don't barge into the tent!' yelled Dad.

Henry pretended he was a hungry Tyrannosaurus Rex.

'OW!' shrieked Peter.

'Henry, don't be horrid!' yelled Mum.

She looked up at the dark cloudy sky.

'It's going to rain,' said Mum.

'Don't worry,' said Dad. 'It never rains when I'm camping.'

'The boys and I will go and collect some more firewood,' said Mum.

'I'm not moving,' said Horrid Henry.

While Dad made a campfire, Henry played his boom-box as loud as he could, stomping in time to the terrible music of the Killer Boy Rats.

'Henry, turn that
noise down this
minute,' said Dad.

Henry pretended
not to hear.

'HENRY!' yelled
Dad. 'TURN
THAT DOWN!'

Henry turned
the volume down
the teeniest tiniest fraction.

The terrible sounds of the Killer Boy Rats continued
to boom over the quiet campsite.

Campers emerged from their tents and shook their
fists. Dad switched off Henry's tape player.

'Anything wrong, Dad?' asked Henry, in his sweetest voice.

'No,' said Dad.

Mum and Peter returned carrying armfuls of firewood.

It started to drizzle.

'This is fun,' said Mum, slapping a mosquito.

'Isn't it?' said Dad. He was heating up some tins of baked beans.

The drizzle turned into a downpour.

The wind blew.

The campfire hissed, and went out.

'Never mind,' said Dad brightly. 'We'll eat our baked beans cold.'

Mum was snoring.

Dad was snoring.

Peter was snoring.

Henry tossed and turned. But whichever way he turned in his damp sleeping bag, he seemed to be lying on sharp, pointy stones.

Above him, mosquitoes whined.

I'll never get to sleep, he thought, kicking Peter.
How am I going to bear this for fourteen days?

Around four o'clock on Day Five the family huddled
inside the cold, damp, smelly tent listening to the
howling wind and the pouring rain.

'Time for a walk!' said Dad.

'Great idea!' said Mum, sneezing. 'I'll get the
boots.'

'Great idea!' said Peter, sneezing. 'I'll get the
macs.'

'But it's pouring outside,' said Henry.

'So?' said Dad. 'What better time to go for a walk?'

'I'm not coming,' said Horrid Henry.

'I am,' said Perfect Peter. 'I don't mind the rain.'

Dad poked his head outside the tent.

'The rain has stopped,' he said. 'I'll remake the fire.'

'I'm not coming,' said Henry.

'We need more firewood,' said Dad. 'Henry can stay here and collect some. And make sure it's dry.'

Henry poked his head outside the tent. The rain had stopped, but the sky was still cloudy. The fire spat.

I won't go, thought Henry. The forest will be all muddy and wet.

He looked round to see if there was any wood closer to home.

That was when he saw the thick, dry wooden pegs holding up all the tents.

Henry looked to the left.

Henry looked to the right.

No one was around.

If I just take a few pegs from each tent, he thought, they'll never be missed.

When Mum and Dad came back they were delighted.

'What a lovely roaring fire,' said Mum.

'Clever you to find some dry wood,' said Dad.

The wind blew.

Henry dreamed he was floating in a cold river, floating, floating, floating.

He woke up. He shook his head. He *was* floating. The tent was filled with cold muddy water.

Then the tent collapsed on top of them.

Henry, Peter, Mum and Dad stood outside in the rain and stared at the river of water gushing through their collapsed tent.

All round them soaking wet campers were staring at their collapsed tents.

Peter sneezed.

Mum sneezed.

Dad sneezed.

Henry coughed, choked, spluttered and sneezed.

'I don't understand it,' said Dad. 'This tent *never* collapses.'

'What are we going to do?' said Mum.

'I know,' said Henry. 'I've got a very good idea.'

Two hours later Mum, Dad, Henry and Peter were sitting on a sofa-bed inside a tent as big as a house, eating crisps and watching TV.

The sun was shining. The sky was blue.

'Now this is what I call a holiday!' said Henry.

HORRID HENRY'S HOME FACT FILE

Parents
Mum and Dad

Brothers
**One horrible
younger brother,
Perfect Peter**

Cousins
**Stuck-up Steve
Prissy Polly
Pimply Paul
Vomiting Vera**

Aunts
**Rich Aunt Ruby
Great-Aunt Greta**

Grandparents
**Grandma
Grandpa**

Pets
**Fang (hamster)
Fluffy (cat)**

Catchphrase
Out of my way, worm!

Hobbies
**Eating sweets
Collecting gizmos**

Pocket money
**50p per week
(much too little)**

Favourite sweets
Big Boppers
Nose Pickers
Dirt Balls

Worst sweets
None

Favourite food
Crisps
Chocolate
Pizza

Worst food
Vegetables
Muesli

Favourite smell
Pancakes

Favourite places
Whopper Whoopee
Gobble and Go
Toy Heaven

Favourite TV programmes
Gross-Out
Rapper Zapper
Mutant Max
Terminator Gladiator
Hog House

Worst TV programmes
Manners with Maggie
Daffy and her Dancing Daisies

Favourite pop groups
Driller Cannibals
Killer Boy Rats

Favourite computer games
Intergalactic Killer
Robots
Snake Masters
Revenge III

Worst computer games
Be a Spelling Champion
Virtual Classroom
Whoopee for Numbers

Best present
Money

Worst present
Frilly pink lacy underpants

Worst punishment
No TV for a week

Greatest ambition
To be crowned
King Henry the Horrible

The HORRID HENRY Books
by Francesca Simon
Illustrated by Tony Ross

HORRID HENRY
HORRID HENRY AND THE SECRET CLUB
HORRID HENRY TRICKS THE TOOTH FAIRY
HORRID HENRY'S NITS
HORRID HENRY GETS RICH QUICK
HORRID HENRY'S REVENGE
HORRID HENRY'S HAUNTED HOUSE
HORRID HENRY AND THE MUMMY'S CURSE
HORRID HENRY AND THE BOGEY BABYSITTER
HORRID HENRY'S STINKBOMB
HORRID HENRY'S UNDERPANTS
HORRID HENRY MEETS THE QUEEN
HORRID HENRY'S JOKE BOOK
HORRID HENRY AND THE
THE MEGA-MEAN TIME MACHINE
HORRID HENRY AND THE FOOTBALL FIEND

HORRID HENRY'S BIG BAD BOOK
a big book of stories about Horrid Henry at school,
with colour pictures and new information –
just like this one!

All the storybooks are available on audio cassette
and CD, read by Miranda Richardson